The
Community

By

S.C. Richmond

The
Community

By

S.C. Richmond

Chapter One

It's late July and hot; Charmsbury Park is looking spectacular with its beautiful floral displays of which the town is so proud. The cordoned off area to the side of the bowling green is the only thing that spoils the view. According to the news this morning on the local radio, a man walking his dog had come across the body of a woman. The official line was that it was natural causes and no-one seemed to have any idea who she was.

Jack knew who she was and was just relieved that the body had been found. He had placed her gently alongside her favourite flowers Geraniums and now her body had been discovered she would get the proper burial that she deserved. She'd been a lovely, kind person, a good friend to him and he was already missing her. He had waited and watched as the police arrived to check the scene and take her body away and he was grateful they had treated her with respect. He had also heard the news play out on the gardeners' radio which was perched on a fence post; it was tuned to a local station that was blaring away whilst he was working diligently at painting some fencing a lurid shade of pink. Now Jack was happy that everything had been taken care of it was time for him to head home and relay the news.

He would have to walk about four miles out of town and get back home without being seen, it seemed like a long walk now that he was almost seventy years old but it would also give him plenty of time to be alone, think and grieve for his friend. He walked past places he knew from his childhood but no one recognized him, he was just another face in the crowd which was the beauty of this being a tourist town and that suited him fine. On his right was the road leading down to the beach, he rarely went there anymore but in his younger days he had enjoyed the beach and on hot summer nights he had slept under the pier, lulled by the sounds of the waves lapping at the sand. Over to his left was a new building that was going to house the new town library, he had read about it in one of the local newspapers but he hadn't yet found out what the old library building was going to be or when the changeover would take place. He supposed it didn't really matter anymore anyway as it had been years since he had needed to use it.

He smiled to himself as the memories came flooding back.

Chapter Two

Jack had been born in Charmsbury on 3rd September 1945 into a wealthy family. Charmsbury was only a small town but being close to the sea it was a popular place for tourists with its hidden coves, sandy beaches and pretty gentle rolling hills just a short distance inland. As a boy it always seemed to him strange and difficult meeting people and becoming friends, then after their two weeks holiday they went out of his life, forever. There was one boy, Peter with whom Jack became the best of friends and they would spend weeks together every summer exploring and doing all the things young boys did, they would write to each other throughout the rest of the seasons but Peter was from way up North so couldn't visit as often as he wanted to. Jack thought of him fondly, they had shared some great times together in fact it was with Peter's help that the doorway had been discovered. It was Peter that got them through the door after working out …..

A horn blasted…. "Get out of the road old man!" The shout jolted him back to reality; he had been daydreaming whilst crossing the road. Not a great thing to do. The driver of the van glared at him in a 'daft old sod' kind of way whilst raising his eyebrows and carried on. Jack knew he really should be more careful not to draw attention to himself, he looked around to see if anyone was watching, just a few concerned glances that were quickly turned away when he made eye contact with them. When he was satisfied no-one was taking any more notice of him, he carried on down the road.

With every step he took the town gradually thinned out and the peace and calm of the Charmsbury countryside started to open up before him, the hills looked like a luxuriant emerald carpet, swaying and dipping in the summer sunshine with just the occasional cloud passing in front of the sun, changing the surrounding colours to a dull olive colour, before releasing the full force of the sunshine on them again. Jack was feeling a little sad for Ruby, she would now have a proper funeral but her friends would not be present to send her off. Although Ruby had known that this was the way it must be, she had seen all of her friends before she passed and she had loved her life, eventually. Ruby had been the sixth person they had put out for burial over the years he'd like a better way to describe it but that was what it was and it always made him wonder if there could have been a better way, that wouldn't eventually lead to their downfall as he knew it most surely would. How many bodies could turn up without someone putting it all together and discovering them? Maybe if his family had been more kind and accepting life could have been very different but they weren't and his life was what it was.

He carefully climbed over a stile, it was rickety with jagged edges from years of use and weather, it had certainly been there as long as he had been alive and probably for many decades before him, he wandered alongside an untidy hedge that bordered the field that for as long as he could remember held numerous sheep. How many times when he was young had he walked here with Mary, holding hands and feeling like he was the luckiest man in the world? Mary had been sixteen, one year Jack's junior when they met in 1962. They played the penny slot machines in the local amusement arcade, he remembered he had tried to tell her that there was a secret to winning on them and then went on to lose all her pennies, he had to take her out to make it up to her; he smiled to himself. The amusement arcade was long gone it had been redeveloped into a pound shop selling cheap gaudy items but life must move forward even if it hadn't changed much for him. Had it been up to him there would be a blue plaque on that wall, the building preserved in the name of romance. He thought then as he still did now that she was the most beautiful, precious thing he had ever seen and she had adored him in return. They thought they would get married and have hoards of children and live happily ever after in a pretty little rose covered cottage but Jack's family had made damn sure that it wouldn't work out that way and Jack was still bitter about it, even after all this time.

He had come from a wealthy family and the relationship had been very much frowned upon from the first moment as Mary was from a local farming family and not a rich one, they considered her not good enough for their boy. They wanted him to marry money and probably wanted to see him married off to the local Solicitor's daughter, there was always money to be found in other people's misery, and for him to keep the family home and textile business going. By 1964 they had made life increasingly difficult for Jack and Mary and she felt she could no longer take the pressure from his family.

He remembered that day like it was yesterday Mary had asked him to meet her in this very field, when he arrived she was leaning against the stile wearing jeans and a pink blouse but her beautiful blue eyes were red from crying, she ran into his arms, pressed her head against his chest and sobbed, she smelt of 'Chance' and it suited her, they held each other for what seemed like an age as if nothing could tear them apart but sadly it already had. They talked for a while and Jack realized he had to grow up and he had to understand that it was too much for her to cope with, his family was making life difficult, trying to stop them from seeing each other and at one stage even offering her family money to stop the relationship but they had liked Jack and wouldn't go along with any of it, instead of accepting the payoff they threw Jacks father out and told him never to return, saying they were not for sale. The pair talked about running away but Mary had been far too sensible for that, there and then he had realized he must allow her to go; her happiness was the price he had to pay. Silent tears rolled down his cheeks as she turned her back and walked out of his life. It was the last time he had seen her; it had been in May 1964.

Heartbroken he stayed in the field all day not knowing what to do or who to turn to, eventually he returned home in the darkness and buried his head in a book and that pattern lasted for months, all he did was read and the only person who could get through to him was his friend Peter, Jack didn't see enough of him for it to make much of a difference. Jack lost interest in anything to do with his family or anything connected to their business, he certainly didn't want a life sitting behind a desk counting the family money. They believed he'd get over it and come back into the fold so they left him to work things out for himself but he never managed to. He spent every spare moment reading English Literature to escape from his real existence. He ploughed through Dickens, Kipling, Stevenson and all of the Bronte's. With his head in a book nobody disturbed him and he could be any character he wanted to be, it was the perfect escape.

He shook himself, reliving all this emotion would help no one, it still made his heart ache viciously in his chest even after all these years the emotions were still as vivid today as they had been then. He wiped away a lone tear from his cheek and kept moving.

Chapter Three

In a farmhouse not far from where Jack was recalling his first love sat a lady reading a letter hand penned from a long lost love.

The paper was a little frayed around the edges and discoloured but it still held the rich creaminess of its quality, the writing was an elegant slanted script marred only by smudges borne from age old tears. Over the years Mary's tears had mingled on the paper with the ones left by Jack when he had penned the letter. The ritual began, she smelt the paper although it held no aroma now her memory could still recall the scent it once contained, he had sprayed the paper with her favourite scent 'Chance', he always used to tell her how good she smelt and she had given him a bottle as a joke so he could smell her even when they were apart. She examined everything about that letter and her heart still felt heavy knowing that this was all that was left of Jack, no-one seemed to know where he had gone all those years ago, she had seen him a couple of times after she walked away from him; ending the relationship, she remembered him doing some work at the library but he hadn't seen her watching him, she had wanted to run to him and hold him but she knew it would break her heart all over again, even though it had been her that finished the relationship she had still loved him dearly and wished they had run away together as he had suggested but as a girl she always had been far too sensible. She slowly read and reread the contents even though she knew the words off by heart, all her emotions feeling as fresh and raw as the day she walked away. She wished she could hold him again.

Mary had had a good life and a great family but there was still a Jack shaped hole in her life, she often read this letter and wondered if her life would have been so very different with Jack than it was with her late husband Geoff. Geoffrey had been a good, honest, hardworking man and had loved her dearly and given her a wonderful family and she had loved him in return although not in the same all-consuming way she had felt about Jack. The trouble was she had never been able to trace Jack after he had disappeared and she had no idea where he was now or even if he was alive or dead; how she regretted finishing their relationship but at the time there wasn't a way around how she felt. She wasn't strong enough back then to fight his family, she was young and didn't know that she should have stood up to them. If she'd have known back then what she knew now she'd have never broken his heart like that.

Chapter Four

Alex Price had been a reporter for five minutes in career terms but was hoping very soon to go further than the lost property section and shop openings on the local paper. She had been training to be a business woman but after writing a short piece on business studies for the local paper whilst she was still at University she had got the bug and decided she could do this for a living. Her parents weren't pleased after she had studied at University for four years and then dropped everything to come home and enter into the world of small town newspapers and she knew nothing about the newspaper industry or about journalism but she loved the challenge, the deadlines and the buzz of the workplace. Much as she was grateful for her job at the paper it wasn't the glamorous job she expected, she'd expected to be picked up by a bigger newspaper and to be interviewing the stars and dealing in Hollywood gossip by now. She was desperate for something more challenging and now she felt her time was coming since she had been chosen to cover the body in the park story for the larger sister newspaper in Wickston as the regular reporter was taking time off to have a baby. A bigger town with a bigger readership, although it was a sad story people wanted to hear about it and know all the whys and wherefores and if she could throw a bit of gossip in too the readers would love it, and she was just the girl to give the readers what they wanted.

What she knew so far, it was a woman's body approximately 50 years old, 5'4", auburn hair cut short, wearing a dark purple long velvet coat over jeans and a T-shirt. She had arrived at the scene just a few minutes after the police and got a good look at the body, no blood, no signs of disturbance or violence. Alex needed an angle but there was nothing much to see, who was she? What was she doing here? How did she die? She snapped a few pictures on her phone so she could take a longer look at them back at the office in case she had missed anything. The Police left with the body and there was nothing else to see, the other reporters didn't seem to have any ideas either, so much for her big break.

Alex wandered off to a local café to get some breakfast and a much needed coffee. The 'Breakfast Bap' was busy this morning and much of the chatter was about the body in the park, she ordered her bacon sandwich and coffee and grabbed the only available seat by the window, the tables here were all close together so she could listen to several conversations at the same time, the trouble was they were all saying the same as she was thinking. Her breakfast arrived.

She had a look through the photos she'd taken zoomed in on every detail and zoomed out again, everything pointed towards the woman having a heart attack whilst she was out but why had she been in the park? There was no worried dog running round on the loose or sat close by guarding its owner, so she didn't have a dog and she noticed that there were no personal affects either. She thought that was odd, if she wasn't out walking the family pet where was her bag? A stereotype she knew but not many women went out for no reason without a bag unless they were exercising and this lady was not dressed for a morning jog. Alex knew it would be the first thing she would pick up when she left the house, now she was beginning to feel like there may be a story after all. She was getting interested and started tuning into other peoples conversations again but there was nothing to be gleaned there. They were just voicing the questions she had in her head, why, where, who?

Chapter Five

Jack was feeling the strain of the day, the heat and the stress had taken its toll and he was fast tiring, it had also been a long time since he had dredged up so many memories. He didn't normally allow himself to wallow in thoughts of the past but today it felt right to reflect on how this had all come about, to remember what had bought him to this point in his life. Ruby's death had reminded him of his mortality. The weather was so warm he felt the need to settle himself down in the shade of an old mature oak tree something that made him feel very young by comparison. As he relaxed he allowed his mind to take him back again to 1964.

That too had been a hot summer although not as warm as this one but then he had seen little of it, he had had his head stuck in classic literature books and enjoyed the escapism of them, an excuse not to face up to what was going on in his life. One day he came across an old family bible and discovered an interest in finding out a little more about his ancestors, where they had come from, what they did and where they had got their hands on enough money to buy the family pile and the surrounding land and which particular ancestor it was that had passed on the belief that few people were good enough to marry into their precious family. Jack had still been angry and was looking for someone to blame. He scanned the names and dates that had been written into the opening pages, all of those people born and died and he knew nothing of them but the family history was all here and up to date he noted as he saw his own name and date of birth just below that of his brother's Jonathon. There were many great aunts, uncles and cousins that he'd never known or even heard of. The bible was very old and incredibly worn and tatty certainly from poorer times when this would have been the only way of documenting the entire family. He had heard stories that it had been Great Grandfather Henry that had acquired the family fortune in 1877 all of the details were a little sketchy but the story went that Henry had won the money, house and some land in some sort of gambling game, the family liked the story but no-one really knew how true it was. The facts were that it all came into the family's possession after old Henry had been out of town for a while. Apparently Henry had been a bit of a wild character, according to family folklore everyone loved him, especially the ladies and no-one would have been surprised if a line of descendants turned up at the house claiming a portion of the family's wealth, good luck Jack thought, you'd never see a penny of this families money. Jack thought he would have liked Great Grandfather Henry had he ever met him it seemed he never let any adventure pass him by if the tales were anything to go by. Wealth for this family had been quite sudden, if it had been due to gambling then the family never took another risk in their history they were not prepared to lose their wealth, it set them apart, allowed them to have the luxury to think themselves a cut above everyone else. Even his brother Jonathon was a snob and a bore and was doing everything possible to live up their fathers ideals, not Jack though he had his own ideas about the way his life should go and he wasn't going to chase the money. Love was what he craved and he had been blessed by finding it with Mary but it was lost all too soon due to his family, now it was time to get as far away as possible from these money hungry, power mad people or be doomed to live as one of them. It seemed that good humour and kindness had left this family when the money had entered it.

Jack had wondered if his heart would ever mend; as he pawed through the old yellowed pages he saw notes scribbled at the edge of the pages, who would draw inside a bible? His family just kept sinking to new lows in his estimation. He continued flicking through it starting to lose interest, the page fell open at Genesis and a mark on the page drew his attention to 50:21.

'Now therefore fear ye not: I will nourish you and your little ones. And he comforted them and spake kindly unto them.'

He began to realize why he had never been drawn to study the bible it was all a bit too cutesy and tongue in cheek for him. When a book could mean so many different things to so many different people he felt that was just too dangerous, there had already been too many deaths over this book. Although at that moment he liked the idea of being comforted and having no fear.

He remembered it all as clearly as if it had been yesterday and looking back it had all been so obvious. He slowly got up and left the shade of the tree into the heat of the unblinkered sun and made his way home.

Chapter Six

Alex was at her desk in the dull newspaper office surrounded only by her phone, computer and several paper cups of cold coffee, she was still waiting for some news from the local police, they didn't seem to be rushing themselves to put a report out, whilst she was waiting she was trawling the internet to try and find some information to put together a story. Facebook did not have a mention of it at all, Twitter threw up a couple of references but they were just locals trading gossip about the unfortunate discovery and there was nothing of any substance. How could it happen that nobody knew who this woman was, why was no one looking for a lost family member or anyone reported missing that fitted her description? Alex felt like she was banging her head against a brick wall. Back to the beginning back to reviewing what she did have, no ID, no signs of violence so not a mugging, no dog, not dressed for exercising, maybe it had been aliens… she had to smile to herself. What was it Sherlock Holmes would have said 'when you have eliminated the impossible, whatever remains however improbable must be the truth.' Maybe it was aliens then. So with no blood and no signs of attack her body must have been moved there after her death. She put out a plea for information on all of the social networking sites, grabbed her bag and her phone and went off to canvass the houses that bordered the park; maybe someone there could have seen something.

It was now mid-afternoon and many of the houses were empty, those that had someone at home either didn't want to talk to her or didn't see anything unusual just the regular comings and goings of the park employees, gardeners, and sport trainers going about their business as usual, certainly no-one had seen a body or anything bulky being taken in or anything out of the ordinary but she hadn't really expected this exercise to turn up anything much, it had been a long shot. She would need to come back later to visit the houses that were at present empty but the inhabitants may have been around earlier in the morning. She decided to walk back to the office as the weather was so nice it seemed a shame to not see at least a little of it, she would be stuck in the grubby office for long enough when information started coming in. She ran her fingers through her hair, put her earphones in and walked in time to 'Don't Stop Believing' her favourite song; she strode out purposefully and enjoyed the fresh air. Her mobile phone beeped just as she was really getting into her stride; here we go she thought as she opened the email from the police.

Chapter Seven

Charmsbury Police

Press Release

Today Wednesday 27th July 2015 at 8.43am

A woman's body was discovered in Charmsbury Town Park by a member of the public.

The body was that of a female, 45-55 years old, Caucasian, 5'4", 140lbs with red hair,   casually dressed.

At this time the victim is unknown.

Cause of death is to be determined but indications are natural, causes we believe she has been dead for approximately 48 hours prior to discovery. A post mortem will be conducted.

If anyone has any information to the identity of the woman please contact your local police station.

Chapter Eight

Almost a day gone and she had to write up a story with the few facts she had, at least now it had been confirmed that the body had been moved to the site but from where and why into the park? She checked her emails and social networking sites and there were no replies to her pleas for help on the internet except for a few cranks on Twitter, strange how the human mind works, the 'I did its' through to alien experimentation, where there's a tragedy a whole spectrum of idiots are sure to follow. The only thing that did catch her eye was a tweet on the Charmsbury feed, all it said was #Charmsbury... Again. She typed in a reply 'what do you mean Again?' And waited.

She wrote up what she knew so far, all fact and nothing to get her teeth into, there seemed to be no gossip surrounding this story yet. She sent the short story through to Charlie the copy editor and hoped she'd have more tomorrow she knew there was a story in it, she could feel it, she just had to find it. There was still no reply on Twitter so it was time to stop relying on others and get some serious groundwork done with only the word 'Again' to go on but it implied there was something to find. She turned to the newspaper archive service and knew this was going to be a long night.

Chapter Nine

Home was cool and welcoming, he was tired after a long day and his legs and back ached fiercely but his friends wanted to know how it had gone as they hadn't heard any news yet. Newspapers when they did arrive were generally a few days out of date and they had none of the new technology to fall back on, mobile phones were expensive, reception was bad and they rarely wanted to contact anyone anyway so news was gleaned when and where possible, normally this was a positive thing but for this event everyone wanted to know what had happened today and in as much detail as he could give them.

Everyone gathered in the recreation area and sat around quietly listening as Jack relayed everything that had happened and a sadness fell over the group, they would all miss Ruby she had always been there with a smile and a kind word when any of them were feeling low and she was a great cook, it was a sad loss to the community. Ruby had been with them for 29 years she had been a tearaway when she arrived but soon found her place in the community, a gentle peace in her life and became a mother figure to the few children that were here. You would often find her playing hide and seek or reading stories she had made up especially for them. Only a few people remembered her coming here as there weren't many people involved with the community back in the 80's and some of them had moved on. Now forty two adults and five children remained and that was about as many as the area could hold, they were mostly good people who came here with a few exceptions over the years but Ruby was special to all of them. They sat together that evening and ate a small simple meal and kept her memory alive, for all the sadness the day had brought it turned out to be a jovial evening everyone had a story to tell, Ruby had got up to many things and made so many people laugh.

Jack made his excuses and slipped away early and slept the sleep of an exhausted man.

Chapter Ten

Going through the archive service for the newspaper was slow tedious work, not knowing where to start Alex decided to work backwards from today and there had still been no reply on Twitter no matter how many times she checked her phone. This work had to be done methodically and slowly as she really didn't know what she was looking for it was like looking for a needle in a haystack. By 9.30pm she had given up, it had been a long day and she really needed to eat, go home and sleep and come back to continue it tomorrow, there had to be a story somewhere or the paper would be sending her back to Charmsbury with a note telling her boss she was useless and to send the cleaner next time as she'd be more useful.

She stepped into her warm flat and headed straight for the fridge and the comfort food, after devouring her favourite snack; pork pie, salad cream and tomatoes she was feeling alert again and ready to do more online hunting. She switched on her laptop and went to make a coffee grabbing a bar of chocolate from the fridge on her way whilst the laptop thought about leaping into action, when it had decided it was ready for her to do some work (they say computers don't have a mind of their own!) She settled back into her comfortable old armchair put her laptop on the worn arm and started searching for the obvious which turned up nothing and then as obscure as she could think of and wait, wait there's something here, a body was found in Topham a small village that borders Charmsbury in 2001, according to the story it was a 47 year old man, Caucasian, who appeared to have been in a fight ending in serious head injuries and was found by the side of the lake, according to the article no-one came forward to claim the body, the police didn't know who he was but he had a tattoo of a football club on one arm and a heart with the name 'Suzi' written through it. The football club tattoo had been Manchester United which had probably been tattooed on men half way around the world she thought, no clue there. A plea had been put out across the UK for any information on him but apart from the tattoos there was nothing to go on. Still maybe there could be a link she thought hopefully; at the moment apart from being unknown they had nothing in common. Alex decided after some sleep she would go and ask the police for some more information maybe they could shed some light on a possible link or they may have at some time in the last(she glanced at the date on the news report Dec 2002, possibly the last time anyone gave that case another thought a last ditch attempt for information before the case was put to bed) thirteen years found out who he was, she would need to ask, another question to add to the list of all the information she was looking for.

Chapter Eleven

9am the next morning Alex drove to the local police station dressed to impress in her expensive royal blue suit that her Mum had bought for her in the hope that the newspaper may take her daughter more seriously if she looked like a smart 1950's lady, to be fair it was a beautiful suit and fitted like a glove and with a white scoop neck T-shirt underneath she felt like she meant business, it gave her a certain confidence that jeans just couldn't do. She hoped it might encourage Inspector Jones to talk to her.

After asking at the desk to speak with him she was kept waiting for over an hour which didn't do her confidence much good but that was the way the police treated journalists, to them she was the lowest life form and as such would have to wait until Inspector Jones just ran out of everything else he had to do before he could be bothered to speak to her. She should be grateful they hadn't just told her to leave but the waiting was tedious, she phoned her boss to let him know why she wasn't behind her grubby little desk and waited. A young fresh faced police woman offered her coffee, she looked too young to be in the police force and made Alex feel older than her years, she gratefully accepted the offer whilst she waited as she figured it may be some time yet, she checked her emails, still nothing of any interest. Then just as the coffee arrived so did Inspector Jones looking for all the world like a modern day Cary Grant, wow this man had presence and even just walking into the public area was played out like a command performance, the noise stopped, the police officers watched him all that was missing was a host of angels to accompany him. She didn't want to look away from this tall, dark vision; she had always loved a man in uniform. "Hello Miss Price, I'm sorry to have kept you waiting, at least they have been looking after you" He glanced at the coffee. His voice was as smooth as his looks, sadly the coffee was not.

"Hello, no problem Inspector, I'm just pleased you could find time to speak with me" It sounded girly and subservient to her ears but at least it was polite and she knew she had to pull herself together or he wouldn't take her seriously. She straightened herself up to her full 5' 3" and looked up at him.

"Please come through to the office, I assume this is about the body in the park" She followed him into a bright, clean but basic office. No photos, no look at how clever I am certificates, just a leather topped desk, a plant and three comfortable chairs. As he sat down and slightly leaned forward she noticed his sparkling green eyes, perfectly smooth skin, clean shaven and a smell of something expensive and musky was wafting off him.

"Yes I've been covering the story and came across something else I hope you could shed some light on" She had found her poise again and continued to tell him all about the information she found online the previous night. It turned out that he knew all about it as some of his longer serving officers remembered working on the case and there was nothing to add to what she knew but he could look into it again, they had never discovered the man's identity and the tattoos had led nowhere, as she suspected. "No dental records?" she added.

"No there was nothing at all that anyone knew about him"

"Surely that's suspicious in itself though isn't it?" She looked him in the eye as she asked the question but had to look away as his good looks were distracting her line of thought.

"We just couldn't turn anything up, yes it was definitely suspicious but if someone doesn't want to be found badly enough, well, there's little we can do, I'm sorry it appears you have had a wasted journey" He stood up, she figured the meeting was over. "I like to work with the press at all times so I hope we can see more of each other, you're quite new to this aren't you?"

"What makes you say that?"

"Normally journalists are much tougher on me than you're being." He laughed and his eyes sparkled "I think we'll get along just fine."

"Is there anything you can give me on the body in the park? Has anything else come up? Do you know who she is yet?" She shut up aware there were suddenly just too many questions there but she wasn't ready to leave just yet. He was already steering her towards the door.

"No we don't know who she is, all we do know is her death appears to be completely natural, a heart attack possibly and she was well dressed and clean so she's been living somewhere, someone will miss her and contact us soon. The only thing we have that was not included in the press release was a piece of jewellery that she had on her, a bracelet made of copper, not expensive or anything just with a weird design on it, nothing I recognized, if you can stop by tomorrow I will get a picture of it for you, unless you'd prefer me to email it." He grinned.

She called his bluff regretting it as soon as the words were out of her mouth "Email is fine, thank you. If there is any connection between these two bodies would you inform me?" She asked hopefully, fully expecting him to laugh at her.

"Of course. I'll keep in touch." Now she could hardly think straight, was he flirting with her? Mum had been right about this suit; she smiled at him as she left.

Only when she was outside the station did she realize she'd been pleasant and sweet and yes he'd spoken with her but she didn't come away with much information, she already knew this was one man that would be very hard to handle, she mustn't let her guard down, she mustn't let him see her swooning over him.

As good as his word Inspector Jones emailed her a photograph of the bracelet and a close up of the design and asked her to contact him if she recognized it from anywhere. Today was a good day.

Chapter Twelve

Jack woke up aching all over, getting Ruby to the park even with the help of Peter and his transport had been difficult and he had walked so far yesterday but now with time everything would return to normal. Peter had not stayed with the others he had to return home, Jack had hardly seen him. Allowing himself to think too much about the old times yesterday had been a mistake he felt like he had a bad case of the blues setting in. He pushed himself out of bed and stretched his aching limbs and attempted to touch his toes, which was normally easy but today he would have to make do with just looking at them, he straightened himself up and looked around him, he was in the same room that he'd lived in for almost 50 years, it was no more than a cave. 13 x 27 feet with a camping toilet in the corner, which he had to clean daily surrounded by a shower curtain for a little privacy although other people rarely came into his room. Old cracking brown and white lino on the floor and a small rag rug, a present from the children for his last birthday they said the bright colours would make him smile every morning when he got out of bed, they were right, even today he found himself smiling at the thought; and an old army bed with a homemade mattress. The stone walls were painted yellow in a vain attempt to brighten the room, no windows, all his light was supplied by a battery lantern when he could get batteries or candles for when he couldn't. His luxuries were books and they were stored reverently in a handmade book case which his oldest friend Peter had made for him and carved so beautifully, this was probably the only truly beautiful thing he owned except of course for the empty round bottle that took pride of place on top of the book case, 'Chance', Mary had given this to him years ago as a joke, so he would never forget her, it had worked, he never had.

On the occasions Peter would still come to stay which became fewer and farther between over the years he would always arrive with boxes full of books, chocolate and batteries for the lamp. Jack was always amazed by their friendship and Peter's thoughtfulness and confidentiality, six decades the friendship had lasted for and his life here would not have been possible or bearable without Peter's help. In times of desperation it was always Peter that came to the rescue, Jack thought about contacting him again and asking for help but he had made his own bed and couldn't just keep expecting Peter to come to his aid, he was beginning to feel like it was time to leave here even after all that he'd built up and the people who now had a reason to keep going. He was tired and wished for a more comfortable life, he knew the end to this way of life must happen for him soon.

He sat down on his bed again and drank a bottle of cool orange juice. He remembered the day he had first come here and the excitement he felt when he realized there was a way out from his family and he realised that he'd found somewhere that was just for him; the penultimate escape.

Chapter Thirteen

It had been late 1964 when he had overheard the head librarian Mrs Sharp speaking to a man in the public library regarding the council giving them some money to redecorate the children's reading room, it was looking dull and tired, the paint in places flaking and they wanted to encourage more young readers in so it needed to be bright, airy and fun. Later that day he spoke to Mrs Sharp about the possibility of him and a friend doing the work but he would need to speak to his friend first, he had never dared to ask her Christian name she was a formidable woman with dark hair pinned up in a bun and a stern face but they got on well as long as he remembered his manners. She said she would consider it. He phoned Peter that evening and asked if he would like to come down to visit and they could take on the work together if Mrs Sharp would give them the job, it would be something to do and they could earn some money so they could have a holiday, the thought of even a short time away from his family always made Jack happy. Peter agreed, so Jack went to see Mrs Sharp with a proposal for painting the reading room and to his amazement she said yes. He hadn't realized it then but she had had a soft spot for Jack and felt sorry for him knowing what his family was like and more importantly she trusted him. So Peter came to visit and they took on the redecoration of the children's reading room, they had a great time and he found he had quite a talent for the work, finally he felt like he had some worth in his own right. They worked from morning to night for seven days, stripping, painting, adding little cartoon characters to the walls and it was when they were on the last part of the job, an old built in cupboard that they had to remove the doors and the casing from, sand the wood down and turn it into a new area for the tots books that they came upon a small wooden door it looked like it was the kind of size that would cover over access to a water tank but the wood looked really old and solid and there was no handle or key hole. They couldn't budge it either and didn't know what to do. So they cleaned it up and polished it and as they polished it revealed a small design, immediately Jack recognized it as the same mark that had been in the family bible, he left Peter and rushed home, grabbed the bible and ran back to the library and sure enough it was the same, they had no idea what it meant but there must be a significance.

They went home that night and tried to decipher the squiggle, they had taken hours over it but couldn't make any sense of it and just as they were about to give up Jack threw the drawing on the table in despair and in that split second the light hit it a different way and he saw it, once he's seen what it meant it was so obvious, it was like a magic picture that was a mass of design but once you stared hard enough it was just a simple picture. It simply read Job 8:8, Job was written in an italic style and when turned on its side they could see the two 8's they turned to the passage and there was the symbol again amongst others.

Job 8:8 - 'For enquire, I pray thee, of the former age, and prepare thyself to the search of their fathers:'

Which meant nothing to them and they had no idea what it could have to do with the door in the library, maybe it was a reference to the family listed in the bible itself but they kept following the changing designs from passage to passage and matching them up, every match signified a different scripture. It was tedious work but it was leading somewhere, so they had to keep going. The next led to Romans 15:4

Romans 15:4 - 'For whosoever things were written a foretime were written for our learning, that us through patience and comfort of the scriptures might have hope'

They had little idea what this could mean; could it be a reference to the library? They moved onto the next indecipherable drawing which after much searching and page turning led them onto

Kings 20:24 - 'And do this thing, take the kings away, every man out of his place, and put captains in their rooms'

Deuteronomy 33:13 - 'And of Joseph he said, Blessed of the Lord be his land, for the precious things of heaven, for the dew, and for the deep that crouches beneath'

By the time they got this far it was getting so late the sun would soon be coming up but they couldn't leave it alone. It seemed that every time they were ready to give up another passage would become evident.

Leviticus 25:19 - 'And the land shall yield her fruit and ye shall eat your fill, and dwell therein in safety'

There still didn't seem to be any sense that they could pull out of these passages. Then the last entry they could find was.

Genesis 19:6 - 'And Lot went out at the door unto them, and shut the door after him.'

It all came together so magically with some effort on their part, after they had discovered the first passage. They had followed the trail to find each one was linked by a drawing or mark of some sort but this was where it seemed to end, there were more marks but they couldn't find any matching drawings to link them to. By then it was almost 8am and they were exhausted it had taken all night but they felt that they must have uncovered something, they had a lot to think about and they had to be at the library by 9am to start work. Not much work got done that day as they pulled and pressed and tried every way they could think of to open the door, for surely according to the scriptures it was definitely a door. They worked their way through the day at a slower pace now to buy themselves more time at the library as well as being tired, then went back to the bible by night to try to discover more information. They tidied and fixed around the doorway whilst they still looked for a breakthrough in the bible passages. A couple of days later at about 2am as they were just about to give up they discovered one more passage that appeared to be linked to the others.

Numbers 21:18 - 'The princes digged the well, the nobles of the people digged it, by the direction of the lawgiver, with their staves. And from the wilderness they went to Mattanah:'

They read them and re read them but they made little sense, then Peter linked Romans 15:4 to the library and they knew they were on to something what they needed was a little lateral thinking. If the first scripture had only been marked to get their interest so the rest must mean something they reasoned, there must be some purpose to the linked scriptures.

Chapter Fourteen

After another dreary story for the paper had been typed up and sent off to Charlie for editing Alex was feeling like giving up, she was so sure there was a story in this but the story for today although on an inner page of the paper really just reiterated what she wrote yesterday, she wouldn't keep the job here unless she turned something up soon. She decided it was time to go back to the archives for an hour or so, there was nothing else she could do.

In 2003 there had been a baby abandoned at Charmsbury cottage hospital, no-one seemed to have come forward with any information about the child. Two days of headlines and it appeared that they gave up looking for anyone. The child had been well looked after and was healthy and happy and adopted by a family that was desperate for a child and were more than happy to spoil this child. She always loved a happy ending.

In 1994 a body had been found on the seafront, a man, natural causes, no clues as to his identity and the body had been put there after death, this sounded almost identical to the body in the park and after a nationwide appeal it turned out to be a man who had gone missing in 1982 from Swansea after a huge family argument and his family had never been able to trace him. According to the headline they said he just disappeared off the face of the earth. Maybe she could contact the family and see if they knew any more about where he'd been for all of those years.

Now she was spurred on and her pulse was racing; she had been looking through the archives for almost three hours but now there seemed to be something to find, the other office workers and reporters had one by one passed by and waved goodnight to her but she couldn't leave this now. That feeling of an imminent story was back. Charlie waved to her and stuck his head over the room divider "Don't stay here all night girl, you're allowed a life too."

"Sure Charlie you have a good evening, I'll pack up here in a while, I think I've got something, just want to check it out."

"What have you found? Do I need to know now or can I go home and leave you to it?"

"Its fine Charlie I wouldn't keep you from your wife, this may not amount to anything yet."

"Goodnight Alex" He got moving just in case she changed her mind and asked for help, the new journalists were always holding him up wanting him to do something and he constantly complained about it to anyone who'd listen. He liked to think of himself as a bit of a father figure, he'd been presiding over this paper for as long as anyone here could remember. He could be grumpy but he secretly had a heart of gold and it was his helpfulness that held him up more than the newbies, he loved everyone to need him, just not too often and only on his terms.

Alex needed to email the information on this missing man to Inspector Jones maybe he had already noted it but maybe not, she wanted to have an excuse to contact him, she definitely wanted to stay on his radar it had been a while since a man had had this effect on her and any excuse to contact him worked for her. She carefully worded the email and hit send. Within two minutes her phone jingled and he had replied, short and sweet it just said thank you. Her stomach sank just a little she had hoped for a bit more than two words that man was really starting to get under her skin. She turned back to the archive screen and carried on a little disheartened.

An hour later she had gone back as far as 1991 and found nothing else, she was tired and she had a local church fete to cover tomorrow for the Charmsbury local paper.

Chapter Fifteen

Jack had spent his morning cleaning the main living area, everyone took their turns in cleaning and cooking, today was no different; once his chores were done he settled down for a rest, everyone else had just gone about their business as usual. He considered the need to go back into town and check up on the news tomorrow, if there was anything to report back it would be easier to pick up a newspaper than have to relay the news, half of which he would undoubtedly forget by the time he got back. He heard the shout summoning everyone for their evening meal and made his way to the dining room, he didn't need to as someone would be kind enough to bring some food to him but he didn't want them to think he was too disheartened so he made the effort. Julie had put together a fantastic meal for them all tonight with their own freshly grown produce and some fresh rabbit that Bob had caught, for a group of people that had little to no money they had some incredible food. Jack looked around at all the faces they looked happy, for some it was the first time in their lives they had found out what happiness meant and they found people who accepted them and cared about them, this truly was a good place. It had evolved by chance but it had turned into a useful peaceful alternative life for many people.

He ate his meal sitting alone away from the main group, they left him to his own thoughts, he was still reflecting on their journey, his mind flipped back to how it had all unfolded; they had at some point realized that they were being pointed towards something below the ground with the help of the bible passages but there was nothing definite in the readings, many times they almost gave up because they just couldn't find anything else to help them work it out but every time they went back to the library and were aware of that small doorway it drove them on to find a solution. They had finished their redecorating of the children's library and they were as proud of their work as Mrs Sharp was pleased. They had even created a mural of cartoon characters on the one plain wall and they had carefully placed a bookcase in front of the small doorway so as not to block it off completely but just enough to keep it as their secret until they worked out what it was for, it was still easy to get access to it if they needed to. On one of their journeys to the library Jack thought it might have been useful to look at the ordinance survey map of the area from 1842, it was incredibly detailed and to his surprise showed a large building where the library now stood but it was far too big to be just the library. He went to see if Mrs Sharp knew anything about this building, she told him that there had been a large and rather grand manor house built here in 1600 but after the Heatheridge family died out the building had fallen into disrepair and been abandoned, it wasn't until the 1920's that anything was done with what was left of the building. The majority of it had been knocked down and the land rebuilt on but a portion of the house was saved and done up as the town hall and this library. He had relayed this information to Peter and their interest in the puzzle was reignited. They went back and pored over the maps again looking for wells as that was the only clue that seemed clear to them but they had never heard of one locally and they slowly searched the map for clues working outwards from the centre of town and eventually they found one a little way from the town on what was now the nature reserve, maybe three to four miles away, they were sceptical as it was so far out of town but that being the only well they could find they decided to go out to the nature reserve and try to find it, if it was still there to find. They didn't want to ask Mrs Sharp too much or she might start asking questions and they may be persuaded to tell her about the door although they assumed she didn't know about it already or surely she'd have mentioned it to them. They took a sheet of paper from next to her typewriter and drew a rough sketch of the area according to the map as Mrs Sharp wouldn't let them take the map out of the library it had 'Reference Only' stamped on it in red and it was more than her job was worth to let it go outside the building. With their drawing and their enthusiasm they went to hunt down the well.

Chapter Sixteen

Her phone tinkled to indicate an incoming email and woke her up, it was still dark, she peered over at the phone it read 5:15am a full hour before her alarm was due to go off. She really must remember to switch it to silent in future. She pushed back the warm, soft duvet and swung her legs out of bed her feet immediately feeling caressed by the sheepskin rug her Mum had bought her to help with cold winter mornings even though it was midsummer she couldn't bear to be without it, it was her idea of luxury. She made for the kitchen, coffee was a necessity this early in the day but then she always had an excuse for coffee. She filled the percolator with water and her favourite coffee and turned her attention to her phone and retrieved the email, the address was showing up as just a row of numbers, great she thought I've been woken up by junk mail, as the percolator gurgled and the smell of fresh coffee washed over her she opened it anyway and it read

Yes. AGAIN. Check the papers 1994, 1990, 1987 & 1979. All unknown. ALL DEAD'

Her heart started beating faster, she tried to reply but the email was instantly returned address unknown. Now she was awake even without the coffee. There was no reference to the 2001 body but then that had been in the next village and may not be linked. She grabbed a cup and poured the hot brown liquid, whilst it was cooling she rushed around had a quick shower, ran a brush through her short blonde hair which normally she was so careful with, threw on jeans and a T-shirt, a swipe of mascara, grabbed her bag and drank back the coffee in one go, switched off the percolator and was gone. She was on her way to the office.

She grabbed another coffee from the machine in the hall on the way to her desk and went straight into the archives it took her nearly two hours to find all the cases that the email had pointed to. She checked Twitter found the 'Again' message and sent another message, this time she took more notice of the original senders account was in the name of John Smith, great she thought the most common name in the country almost untraceable unless he contacted her again. The information under his name was left blank and his profile photo was just a picture of fields. Without a computer whizz kid at hand she knew she could never trace 'John Smith' and for some reason it seems he didn't want to be found. If she couldn't find anything herself she would get the IT boys in they would have a go at finding him for her.

She phoned Inspector Jones to relay the news but he wasn't at his desk so she left a message. She hoped he would return her call before she started on her new story because she might just be on the wrong track also she wanted to hear his voice again. He might even ask her to go and see him to explain her findings; she was more than just a little bit smitten.

Now she had the previous cases she had discovered and another three to add to the equation, all unknown, two women, clean, tidy, no ID, no unusual distinguishing features and all of them except one had been moved to where they were found at least two days after their deaths. She wondered now if the baby was part of it too although apart from being unidentified there was nothing else there to point to it being linked to the deaths. All except for one had been found in the town of Charmsbury and only one of the bodies had been claimed by their families. All missing persons cases. That's it, she was so pleased she had found a connection of sorts; the connection was they were all unconnected. The link was they were all missing people but that opened up other questions, what were they doing in Charmsbury, what drew them there?

She made the church fete with minutes to spare, truth be told she'd almost forgotten about it with all of her excitement. The fete was a success and she would report it as a triumph, mention a few local dignitaries, that always went down well and get back to her big story, her mind was totally taken up with everything she had discovered today.

She headed back to her desk and settled down much happier now she had a far more interesting piece to write for the paper unless Inspector Jones called and stopped her; just a small part of her now hoped he wouldn't contact her too quickly, unless it was for a date of course.

Chapter Seventeen

It was a cool hazy morning on the hills and Jack's favourite time of day; the trees in the distance looked like all their edges had been softened as they gradually blended into the sky and they had a quietness about them that always bewitched him it was so beautiful out here; he breathed in the fresh air filling his lungs to almost bursting point and releasing his breath slowly, savouring the moment, tasting the air. He chose to start out early this morning, he hadn't slept well worried by thoughts of change and hoped the beauty of his surroundings may give him a different aspect on things; he seemed to have so much on his mind. He stretched, arching his back and then returning to touch his toes which was still difficult but the ache was easing he would be fine again by tomorrow, he leant against a low stone wall to stretch out his legs one at a time just like an athlete would, not bad for an old 'un he thought and smiled. As he pushed away from the wall surrounding the well he paused and thought yes, yes we did find the well didn't we.

It had taken them several days to actually find it but when they did it had been overgrown and in dire need of cleaning out but it certainly was a well and they were excited about it and also a little curious as to why nobody else knew about it. The wall around it had crumbled away mostly but once they had set to cleaning it up and removing the debris of leaves, stones and mud that had amassed inside and blocked the flow, it bubbled up and offered fresh clean spring water, after a day or two they were brave enough to drink some and it had been cold, crisp and sweet, he remembered it like it was yesterday he could still recall that first sweet taste. The natural well had been one of the most amazing things about this place and they set about gathering stones and building the wall back up to contain the spring a little; it had been messy and fun work. This had become the place that Jack spent most of his time and apart from Peter no-one knew where to find him; it seemed that nobody ever came here and the few people he had spoken to knew nothing about any natural springs or wells in the area. Now he had found his private place and he would come out here most days to just be away from everyone and to sit and read. That had been 50 years ago and he still enjoyed it here now and often he still bought a book out here, leant against the hand built wall and read.

Fully stretched and feeling good Jack started the walk into Charmsbury to find out if there was any news on Ruby, he wouldn't go through the field today he differed his route every time he went into town so he wouldn't be noticed, not that he went into town very often but enough that if he wasn't careful he would be. There was a small shop on the edge of town where he could have picked up a newspaper and it was much closer but it was the sort of place where people liked to chat and know your business, a typical English village attitude, so he would have to go into the bigger stores in the town centre where the staff always looked bored and like they wanted to be anywhere else but at work and they wouldn't notice you if you had two heads so long as you had the right money so they didn't have to do anything; and that suited him fine.

Chapter Eighteen

Alex was proud of her story, she had worked hard at it and although it contained a lot of speculation it made for good reading. Charlie must have thought so too because he'd moved it up to page three, she was hoping that she could keep the story running at such a good pace until the police worked out who the body was, which meant a lot of work today to find a fresh angle. Now she was assuming that all the deaths were of people who had gone missing for one reason or another, maybe it was time to go and quietly mingle with the people on the street, see if they had heard anything about bodies turning up in the town. She printed off photos of all of the bodies and trimmed them down to just faces so as not to freak anyone out, she wanted answers she didn't want to depress people who were already down on their luck. It was definitely a jeans and T-shirt day today, she took some money too just maybe she'd have to stump up for a meal or two and more than a few cans of special brew. Whatever it takes to get a story she thought and grimaced at the tacky cliché.

She headed down towards the river end of town, the local council had 'cleaned up' as they liked to call it the seafront area, they didn't like the idea of all those tourists bringing all their money to town then seeing the down side of town life, god forbid, they may take their money elsewhere and that just wouldn't do. Keep it sparkly and pretty so that everyone feels safe and believes that nothing bad could ever happen in this town, they even went to the trouble of employing a tour guide dressed as a Victorian policeman to walk round the streets, you could often hear the American tourists 'Oh my, will you just look at that, how quaint. We must get a picture?' These tourists were so easily pleased but they rarely got to see the other end of the spectrum down by the river, only a five minute walk away, where regularly you could find people sleeping under the bridge and gathering around each other whilst they handed out their little parcels of amphetamines and lumps of cannabis resin and far, far worse. Alex didn't want to get involved but knew that it may be the only way to get her new angle on this story. She waited by the side of the bridge too frightened to go under it with the dealers and the drunks, she would try and catch one or two when they came out, hoping they'd be in a good enough state to hold a conversation with her. She heard shouting from under the bridge, men's angry voices and a woman yelling for something to stop. She waited, the first person to emerge from under the bridge was a young guy and it looked like he'd been in a fight, there was blood drying on his dirty face and his hands looked red raw as if he's been punching a brick wall, she really didn't want to see the state of the other guy. Alex stepped back; she didn't think she was up to talking to him; he scared her, she could feel her own fear bubbling up and she took a step closer to the road back up to where there were more people; he looked her up and down and grinned at her but there was no warmth in the grin "Looking for a bit of rough cutie?" he growled but he kept moving. She was sweating; this is stupid she thought, I can't do this, why did I ever think I could. A woman wrapped up in several layers of what looked like rags appeared next and acted like Alex wasn't there or at best an inconvenient obstacle, she pushed past Alex without a word, Alex stumbled against the wall, righted herself and turned on her heels feeling scared and ashamed maybe she should just leave it to the police now she knew she was out of her depth before she'd even really got started.

She returned to the office, where she felt safe amongst people she was getting to know. She sat down heavily in her chair and wondered what to do next.

"What's up Alex, you look like you've seen a ghost"

"Bad morning Charlie, I think I've bitten off a bit more than I can chew, I'm going to check the archives again" She turned on the computer whilst talking to him, she felt calmer in front of a computer screen.

"Sure you're OK?" He truly sounded concerned "Anything I can help with"

"Thanks Charlie I'm fine, just a bad morning" She put a big smile on and turned towards the screen. She felt defeated and cowardly, now she was back at the office she felt a bit stupid, the guy hadn't hurt her or even shouted at her and the woman had only pushed past, worse happened when she was at the supermarket. She needed to get a grip of herself and get the job done. She didn't mean to shun Charlie but he was so kind to her she felt like she would cry if he pushed her.

She spent the next forty minutes writing up her story on the church fete, feeling like maybe this was far more like the kind of reporting she was cut out for. With that done she felt calmer and a little more like her normal self, it was time to move on with her main story.

She decided to try and canvass the houses that were empty last time she did a door to door and she needed to speak to the police to try to find a way to contact the man who had found the body but she could waste another hour here on the archives before doing anything else. She didn't find anything else but she didn't feel like she was really looking, she really needed to pull herself together.

Chapter Nineteen

He knew it had to happen eventually. He had decided to walk through the town park, he knew he shouldn't as he was only here a couple of days ago but he hoped nobody would notice him, he could just be another holidaymaker taking a stroll before breakfast. He had luck on his side this morning he hadn't needed to purchase a newspaper, when he walked through the park there was a discarded local rag folded up on a bench, he was glad he didn't need to walk any further and sat down to see if there was any news on Ruby, he didn't expect there to be but he just wanted to be certain that there were no complications. Nothing on the front page which in his mind made everything okay, then he opened the paper and the headline hit him like a freight train, in big bold black print.

'MISSING PEOPLE TURN UP DEAD'

His skin immediately turned cold and his heart started beating hard in his chest, he wasn't sure his ribcage could contain it any longer, he was sweating and his vision blurred a little, come on he thought this is no time to have a heart attack. He took some deep breaths and steadied himself he was okay it was just panic or fear this time; his heart was fine he forced himself to calm down, slowly he started to return to a state of normality.

When he had composed himself, he looked around, there was no-one about, no-one looking his way with concerned glances, it had all happened internally thankfully. He returned his gaze to the headline with the name 'Alexandra Price' the author slightly below it, okay it wasn't much of a headline but the journalist had got too close for his comfort. He read on and realised that it was pretty accurate but the way it was written it seemed the journalist wasn't sure, she was taking a chance on printing this and wouldn't quite commit herself to some of the facts almost like she needed a story and although she had linked things together well she was only guessing at things, there was nothing here that he needed to worry about too much, no proof, unless she kept digging and came up with anything else. This wasn't as bad as the headline had initially made him think it would be, he would have to watch this journalist he thought as he made a mental note of her name 'Alexandra Price'. He realised that he would be doing a lot of walking over the next few days, he could let one of the younger guys do the running around for him but he didn't want to worry anyone else with this, but he needed to keep an eye on how close anyone was getting to them because if this was how a journalist was thinking surely the police were thinking it too.

Jack folded the paper up and tucked it under his arm and sauntered over to the area where the grounds man had been listening to his radio last time he was here, if he was lucky he could catch the local news on the radio, today there was no-one around and he couldn't hear a radio playing anywhere.

He thought he should walk back and try to tune their little portable radio in and see if this news had gone any further. It was an old and battered Hitachi transistor radio in an equally battered leather case but it worked, young Jess had bought it with her when she settled with them and left it for them as something to remember her by when she decided it was time to move on, she'd stayed for a couple of years but eventually decided it was time to go home and make things up with her family. People didn't often leave once they'd been welcomed into the community but if they decided to make a go of things with their life they were encouraged to, there could be a great life and much love to be had back in the outside world. Jack just asked that they never mentioned where they had been to anyone else however much they wanted to, he wanted to keep the people that remained there safe and away from people that may wish to do them harm.

They didn't like to use the radio too much as they were always low on batteries so it was saved for occasions when they really needed to know something, or when they were having a celebration of some kind and wanted some music other than the music they made amongst themselves, sometimes they would hear a song on the radio then the musical housemates would go into a huddle and come out playing it on their basic homemade instruments, except Carl who had turned up with a guitar slung over his shoulder it was his pride and joy, he thought himself a bit of a rock star and to the rest of the community he was. It never sounded anywhere near the same but everyone had a lot of fun listening to them adlibbing to the latest songs and would dance around whirling and jumping in time to the beat.

Chapter Twenty

Mary was sitting in her comfortable luxury tan leather armchair; she had treated herself a year ago when she had a small win on the lottery and she loved to sit and read the paper and do the Sudoku challenge with her feet up and a cup of tea. Today was a special occasion, she was reading the story that the new girl at the paper had put together. It was a clever story and must have taken some imagination and it certainly grabbed the reader. A woman's body found in the park, what was happening in this town, it used to be so quiet here but Alexandra Price had made the town sound like it was all set to appear in an episode of CSI. Mary vaguely remembered a couple of incidents in town but wouldn't have thought to connect them, it all happened over such a long period of time. The paper and its readers would always love a conspiracy theory though and it would give the locals something to talk about for a while. If Alexandra was lucky maybe a national paper would pick it up but so far not even the local radio station had. Mary thought she should get the story first-hand as it would be a great talking point at the next book club meeting.

Mary leant over picked the phone up and dialled the 'Daily News'.

"Hi Charlie, how are you? What are you doing answering this phone? Nothing to do?"

"Mary, great to hear from you, our star reporter's just off getting a coffee, hang on, she's on her way back now." She could hear him hand the phone across and imagine him mouthing her name. Mary had always liked Charlie.

"Hello Alex, your story's causing a bit of a stir I gather, you'll be snapped up by the tabloids soon if you carry on like this."

"Aww Nan you're just biased, did you really like it?" Mary could hear the smile in Alex's voice.

"Of course I did but I don't know where you got your imagination from, pulling info from all those years ago and linking them all, great story but you know me I need more info, your nosey old Nan wants the inside scoop. So when are you coming to see me?" Mary chuckled, she knew that would wind Alex up and then she would have to visit to tell her the whole story.

"Ok, I get it, you want gossip for one of your meetings, you got it Nan and it's not imagination, this is all for real. I'm sure. I'll be round later. Thanks for ringing." Alex hung up and smiled. She loved her Nan and was sure that was where she got her nosiness from. She loved to get all the gossip before her cronies did and having a granddaughter on a newspaper was like having her own inside line.

Alex always felt better after she'd spoken to her Nan but now she needed to get away from her desk and go and knock on some doors, this was going to be much more pleasant than her attempt at tough grass roots reporting earlier today. She was still feeling like a coward in addition to feeling a bit stupid for running away. What had she expected? She needed to toughen up a bit otherwise she'd get nowhere.

She drew a blank on the door to door search for information but a lovely elderly lady called Rose had talked to her about the comings and goings daily at the park, there was nothing that could help her story but the endless supply of tea and cakes had been a very welcome addition to the chat, she might just have to mention that she had a source overlooking the park, not much for an hours work but it might add a little intrigue to her story.

She needed to get hold of Inspector Jones next to see if he had any news or could give her details of the man who found the body. Any excuse to speak to him at the moment would be good, she could do with his kind of distraction from work and she was also curious to know what he'd made of her story, she hoped for admiration but expected amusement.

Chapter Twenty One

Inspector Matthew Jones was sitting at his desk having read the paper, he was going to have to speak to Alex again because either she knew something he didn't or she was trying to scare the people of Charmsbury, he hoped it was just a story to keep people picking up the paper because if any of what she had written was true his force would be a laughing stock. He really hoped the officers working on this case either already knew about all the incidents being linked and were working on it or had already discredited that line of thought. He would have to contact her and see what she was thinking of writing next, he had really liked Alex when he met her but now he was beginning to think she could be trouble. Although cute troubles like her he thought he could handle. He set about sending her an email.

He called in the officer in charge of the case one PC Dave Collins to get fully up to date, PC Collins had seen the story too and had been checking her facts and he thought it was possible that the incidents could be linked but they didn't have enough evidence to make it all hang together, they were trying to contact the family of Joe Evans, the body that was found on the seafront in 1994, to see if they could offer any information but he thought it would be a waste of time. PC Collins was quite sure that this was just a story and although it would be a convenient way to link the victims he didn't think it really worked, there was just not enough evidence for them to go on.

Matthew sat down and waited for a reply to his email, he was sure it wouldn't be long they both knew they were attracted to each other it was only a matter of waiting to see who'd make the first move. The moment he'd first set eyes on Alex he had been hooked but he was trying to play it cool. He was a police Inspector and she was a journalist, it was like oil and water, they shouldn't mix, they just couldn't mix but he didn't know how long he could keep her at arm's length. If it did work out it could spell either the end of her career or his and he was sure that neither of them wanted that to happen.

His phone rang "Miss Price for you sir."

"Put her through." He waited for the click signifying connection.

"Hello Alex, you got my email then, thanks for calling."

"Hi, no I haven't had an email I just needed to speak to you about the gentleman that found the body, can you give me his name and contact details?" He bristled at her brazenness and by the fact that super-fast technology was no better than snail mail.

"Sorry Alex, I can't give you that information, it's an on-going investigation, I'd love to help but my hands are tied, sorry." He wasn't sorry at all and they both thought it at the same time but there was nothing else to be said. He definitely wasn't going to get a date by talking to her like that and she didn't appreciate the brush off.

"Ok, thanks anyway. Just thought I'd try. By the way what did you email me for?"

"Where you got your information for your story? So do you want to tell me?"

"No, that'll be privileged information from my sources." She had to smile to herself because she knew that he knew had he been less severe they could have shared information, not that she had a lot to share anyway but he didn't need to know that, well not just yet.

They stiffly said their goodbyes. Matthew could have kicked himself; he knew he should have handled that better. He'd really have to up his game with this woman; it appeared that she was more than a match for him and that only made him want to get to know her more. He reluctantly placed the phone back in its cradle.

Chapter Twenty Two

There had been nothing about the story on the radio news at all, Jack relaxed and thought it would all be okay. He would wait a couple of days before going to check up on the journalist again. Everything was going to return to normal again and that was good for everyone. He had to wonder if this Alexander Price could find out anything else about them, over the years one or two people had come close to finding them but that was more luck than judgement on their part but no-one had ever really found anything out about them, nor as far as he knew was anyone interested in looking. To date the only people who knew about the community were people who had been invited in and they were few and his brother, well that was another story altogether.

It had all started in reality whilst he was sitting by the newly discovered well and he was admiring the handiwork on the well wall, his mind turned back to the scriptures and the doorway in the library, how could they be linked because they surely were. To date the bible passages had led him and Peter to the well that had been linked to the doorway and he was certain the others would lead him somewhere too. He looked out over the land with its gentle rise and fall of the grass and wild flowers. He was aware that long ago this had all been farmland before it had been swallowed by the wildness of nature, maybe which was what the 'nurturing' and 'eating your fill' references were all about. He looked around and thought the whole area must have been completely flat at some stage but he supposed the land had settled in places and given the land its bumps and dips he could see now. Bushes had grown clumped together and entwined, nature truly had taken over this area with no human intervention over the years, some of the nature reserve was cared for but this side of the reserve had been left to fend for itself. Jack had never understood why.

He had got up and walked around the area and studied the plants and flowers, took a look at the crowded bushes, they were brambles which were still holding onto a few white flowers but there were also small green new blackberries, it looked like there would be a lot of fruit on these bushes in a few weeks, he pushed his way into the brambles to get a better look at the fruit, the brambles scratched him, the branches caught him and the thorns hooked his skin and tried to hold him, he pushed on he was determined to see just how much fruit these bushes were loaded with. His mind stopped him in his tracks 'The land shall yield her fruit and ye shall eat your fill, and dwell therein in safety' it was one of the scriptures, he couldn't remember which one but he remembered reading it only the evening before. He forgot about the scratches from the brambles and pushed his way deeper into the darkness of the bush, he didn't know what he expected to find but he wasn't going to give up until he found some sort of explanation, he wove his way around the bushes long canes and through the lush green leaves, glancing down at his arm he knew the bush had taken its revenge on his trespassing through it, he could feel the trickle of warm liquid on his wrist. There was more fruit there than he was ever going to be able to eat, his foot bumped into a mound of grass, raised to about 2 foot above the ground and approximately five feet around, there was also a lot of moss covering the mound and he could make out the outline of large lumps of wood, he stepped up onto it only to scratch his head on the upper brambles and then he sunk down a little, it made him wary of stepping forward again he couldn't see what he was stepping on or into it was too dark amongst the brambles. He needed more space and more light.

The following day he had returned with a torch, a pair of secateurs, gloves and a small garden trowel, he swore the bush would not win this time. He cut his way in trying not to do any damage to the bush and found the mound once again, he scraped away at the moss and found stone below it, when he'd cleared most of the moss the stone was in a circle with a dip in the middle, he wedged the torch in the brambles and dug, wishing that he'd brought a spade with him. He dragged out mud, leaves, dead wood and more than a few insects, they were scattering in every direction now he'd disturbed them, it hadn't taken him long to discover a hole and from what he could see with the torch it looked deep. He had run home full of excitement and phoned Peter telling him to get the next train down he had something to show him.

Chapter Twenty Three

Peter had turned up the following afternoon, Jack had shown Peter the bible passage, then they collected up more batteries for the torch and a few small tools just in case they needed anything, just things they could get in their pockets, Jack had left his backpack there the day before with the things he had taken then. He knew he didn't want to draw too much attention from his parents so he had stashed his bag inside the brambles and was only seen to leave home with books and drinks. He was excited to be showing this to Peter although at that time he hadn't even begun to imagine what secrets the brambles would hold.

They worked hard, moved large chunks of wood that were damp with moss and with every movement they disturbed hundreds, maybe more like thousands of insects that scurried off to find somewhere else damp and dark. They cleaned out the area back as far as the stone but they still couldn't find the bottom of the hole, they stood over the hole they had excavated with their few tools and their hands and looked down in amazement. Jack shone the torch in but the light wasn't strong enough to find an end to it, the light picked up the walls that gently dipped down into the earth, they looked at each other with a mixture of disbelief and excitement, it was Peter that put it together with the scriptures he whispered almost as if he were just thinking out loud "the deep that crouched beneath" he took a deep breath "this is what it meant"

They sat on the edge of the hole and pushed themselves in, it was damp and smelt of rotting vegetation but it wasn't so much a hole as a gradual slope just a short drop from the opening, and then if they ducked their heads they could just about stand up and walk. With great trepidation they had inched forward aiming the torch at everything in turn, walls, floor and ceiling. The floor was dirt and stones like an old gravel track, the walls were stone and wood, well-constructed, reinforced and looked incredibly sturdy, the ceiling the same and they could hear small animals scurrying about as they caught the smell and vibration of intruders in their home. There were spider's webs everywhere; this was a whole new type of nature reserve. They were dumbstruck, this was amazing "where do you think it goes?" asked Peter in a reverent whisper, he was so lost in the moment he physically jumped when Jack replied. In truth they had no idea but they were both thinking that this couldn't possibly have anything to do with the door in the library, they were just too far away from town although the scriptures were leading them to believe it was. They moved forward slowly through the tunnel to a place where it forked, now which way should they go? This was much bigger than they could have ever believed or hoped, they turned towards the left hand wall and walked forward, it didn't go far it ended in a bulbous area maybe a small room or a storage area. They backtracked to the main tunnel and decided they should go back out to the fields, they needed to map the tunnel, if there were any more turn offs in the tunnel they could soon get lost if they weren't careful. They made their way back towards the entrance, scrambled upwards and hoisted themselves out. It was much easier to get in than to leave. They left their tools in the backpack and dropped it just inside the tunnel entrance and made their way back to Jack's house.

They used the rest of the day to collect together all of the items they could possibly think of that they would need to make a map including another torch, even more batteries, a small paraffin lamp with extra paraffin and new wicks, gloves, sketch books, pens, pencils, compass and a small battery run clock so they could keep an eye on the time, if they were out too late Jack's parents might ask too many questions as it was they were lucky they left the two boys alone most of the time. All the items were carefully packed into Jacks old Adidas sports bag ready for an early start the next day. Not that they got much sleep that night, they sat up talking into the early hours full of excitement, they fell asleep around 3am exhausted.

Chapter Twenty Four

Alex followed the smells of baking to Mary's door, whenever she came to visit there was always homemade cakes and biscuits still warm from the oven. They settled into the cosy smelling kitchen and whilst drinking wine and eating chocolate cake Alex told Mary everything she had found out for her story and Inspector Jones reaction to her information.

"So Matthew didn't think much of your story then?" Mary asked with a slight smile.

"Who's Matthew?"

"The Inspector you've been talking about for the past half an hour."

"Matthew ..." She pulled herself out of her mini daze "Do you know everybody in town Nan?"

"No, just the nice women and the handsome men, you like him don't you?"

"Yes, I mean he's ok, but he makes me feel dumb every time I speak to him."

"Oh... You really do like him." Mary smiled knowingly, Alex always had worn her heart on her sleeve and Mary hadn't heard her talk so much about someone of the opposite sex for a long time, in fact since she left university and her then boyfriend, to come back to Charmsbury and work for the local newspaper.

"Nan!" Alex blushed. "But as you ask I don't think he cared for my reporting one little bit, I don't know if that means I'm on the right track or not but I need to keep looking into it. You know everyone around here, anything unusual over the years that could be connected?"

"Nothing I can think of, there's strange things that happen in all towns but generally nothing sinister, there was that baby that was dumped at the hospital years ago, no-one ever found out where she came from but I don't know how that could tie in, we don't get too much gossip around here." She paused, a slight smile on her face. "...and I hope you didn't give that Rose too much information... she's one of the members of our reading group, and I don't want her getting to the good stuff before I do, I've got a reputation to keep up". They both laughed knowing there was more than a little truth in that statement.

"Do you know the girl who was adopted?" Alex was curious again now.

"No, I don't know how that slipped past me but it was all kept very quiet, I'm sure it was a local family but I don't know if they're still here or who they were in the first place. There were lots of young families around here at the time" She gazed off into nowhere. "Some things we never find out if they don't want to be found."

Alex looked at her Nan, at 68 she was still a handsome woman with a heart of gold and she wondered what her life had really been like; everyone in town seemed to admire her and wanted to bask in her shadow just a little bit but in her moments alone was she happy or was she lonely since Granddad had died? She had lived in Charmsbury all her life, she had the chance to leave several times, Granddad had always wanted to move away so they had to compromise and have lots of holidays but still live here because Nan wouldn't leave, this was her home town and this was where she wanted to be. Alex didn't really understand that, she herself would love to move away to some other part of the country or even the World; she certainly didn't want to spend her whole life in small-town Charmsbury.

"Why did you always want to stay here Nan? Did you never think it may be nicer somewhere else?" Curiosity had got the better of her, she had to ask.

"This is where I fell in love Alex, how could anywhere be better than that?"

"Do you still miss him?" Alex asked thinking about her Granddad.

"I've always missed him" Mary replied although she was aware that they were talking about different people. The conversation dwindled after that, Mary was thinking about Jack.

Alex made her excuses; Mary loaded her up with cakes and biscuits and hugged her goodbye. Alex wanted to head home, she needed to come up with a way to keep her story alive and with no new information that was going to take some imagination as there was no gossip to be gleaned from her Nan. She thought that maybe she should take a look at the baby information again and see if there was anything else to find out, somebody somewhere must know what happened to the little girl.

What she actually did when she got home was kick off her shoes, settle into her favourite old armchair and fall asleep.

Chapter Twenty Five

The boys had chatted all the way to the tunnel the next morning they were so excited, they had made themselves a bag full of cheese sandwiches and picked up a couple of bottles of fruit juice, their bags were feeling heavy by the time they got through the brambles and to the tunnel opening but they didn't care, they had to get as much done in the following two days as they could because Peter had to go home, his Dad had found him a few days' work at the factory he worked at and was hoping it might lead to a full time job for his boy. Peter on the other hand hated the idea of working in a factory but would do a few days' to please his Dad. So there was no time to lose. They checked their compass, changed the torch batteries, picked up their bags and went down into the tunnel. They counted their steps as they went along, not sure how else to judge the distance. Their voices sounded weird in the tunnel, one, two, three they sounded dull as if the walls were absorbing the sound instead of carrying it and the smell of damp old earth was overpowering, they got to step ninety seven and that brought them as far as the fork in the tunnel, they turned left, thirteen steps took them to the area they thought of as a storage room, they stopped and sat down on the dirt floor, noted the distances and drew a crude map. This area was small, they had to sit with their backs leaning against the wall with their legs straight out in front of them, their feet almost touched the opposite wall. With the map up to date they walked back to the main tunnel and this time turned left into unknown territory. Clearing vast spider's webs along the way and brushing away clumps of mud from the walls they noticed the ceiling was getting a little higher, they no longer had to watch their heads, they continued on for another 137 steps and saw another tunnel leading off to the right. This tunnel was only five steps long and led to an area much larger than the first; they stopped again to update their map and lit the paraffin lamp so they could see the whole room instead of just parts at a time with the torch. This room even had shelves on the wall on one side of the room, they were made of wood and obviously very old because when they touched them they rocked against the wall a little and it felt like they might bring them all crashing down. They felt damp and rotten; spiders scurried up the walls to escape the invasion.

They couldn't believe how big this tunnel was, they walked on it weaved and dipped a little, their direction changing all the time, they stopped in convenient areas to update the map although the directions all seemed wrong on paper. By the time they had walked approximately two thousand steps they had discovered four smallish rooms, one large and one huge room with another tunnel leading to yet another small room, and they could see that the tunnel went further ahead but they had to call it a day and get home. This time they left all of their things in what they were calling the 'storage room' now they were confident that it was safe in the tunnel and just took an empty bag back, they would fill it with more items that evening that they may need to continue investigating.

By day two they were covering the area more quickly and moving around the tunnel with much more confidence, they discovered a distance up to seven thousand steps and an additional fifteen rooms of varying sizes, there was another smaller tunnel that had been a dead end, blocked by stone and rubble but it didn't look like it had collapsed it looked like it was just a dead end. Jack knew he would be back the next day to check that over properly, he wished Peter could stay longer there was so much more to explore.

Peter had gone the next morning promising to return as soon as he could to continue the mapping of the tunnel, they swore each other to secrecy but Jack knew he wouldn't wait for Peter, he would keep returning until he knew everything about this discovery. Soon the storage room began to fill up with tools, books and no end of useful items. After eight days Jack had as far as he knew fully mapped the tunnel and come up against two dead ends and a total of twenty six rooms all within approximately nine thousand steps, some rooms were only accessible from going through other rooms, it was a real maze. He had no idea what it was for or why it was here.

Chapter Twenty Six

She went to the hospital to see if there was any information or gossip to be had about the baby who she now knew was a girl thanks to her Nan. The girl would be about twelve years old now so that narrowed the search, if they were still in town.

At the hospital Alex looked around for an older member of staff but they all seemed so young. There was an information desk by the entrance but no-one was sitting behind it, she stood there for a few minutes thinking about what she should do next.

"Alexandra?" The voice cut through her thoughts. "You were in a daydream there weren't you" This was a statement not a question. "What can I do to help you today?"

Alex turned around towards the voice and saw the small frame and white hair of Rose, the lady who lived by the park and made excellent cakes. She said a silent thank you to herself and any ethereal hosts who may have been listening.

"Hello Rose, I was hoping to find someone in the maternity ward who may have worked here in 2003, can you point me in the right direction?" She mentally crossed her fingers and waited.

"Oh you must be wanting to know about that poor abandoned baby, although I don't know why you'd want to, nobody knows anything here but I suppose you could speak to Patty she's been working here since the nineties and delivered more babies than I've had hot dinners. You'll find her in the office just down the hall to the left."

"Just want a chat." she told Rose honestly "don't know what I'm looking for at the moment, will she talk to me?" and as an afterthought "how did you know? Hasn't anything memorable happened here apart from an abandoned child in 2003?" Rose chose to ignore the sarcastic remark.

"Patty could get Olympic gold in talking so don't worry about that, whether she's got anything useful to say is another matter. Just tell her you're a friend of mine and let slip who your Nan is, she'll be fine." Rose smiled at Alex showing a full row of her perfect white dentures. Rose was turning out to be a real sweetheart.

Alex walked down the corridor as instructed and found Patty straight away, she was a tall, rotund woman with the most welcoming smile Alex had ever seen, she had to wonder how long that would last when she started asking questions. "Hello, I'm Alex. Rose sent me down to see you."

"Well come in Alex, now you're obviously not about to give birth, so what is it I can do for you?" She beamed at Alex and Alex immediately understood why people wanted this woman to be their midwife, she could make you believe giving birth was as painless as popping out to lunch with friends. Alex was instantly at ease in her presence and quickly decided that honesty was the way to go with Patty "I've come to ask for some information on a story I'm looking into. I'm with the Daily News." She hesitated then remembered what Rose had told her. "Rose mentioned you might know my Nan, Mary?"

"Oh my, you're Mary's clever granddaughter, she's always talking about you, you make her very proud and I know you of old Alex, even though we haven't met for what is it... 23 years?"

Alex just looked at her not knowing what to say.

"I was your Mum's midwife when I first started here, so it's nice to meet you again and see you all grown up, just so you know I was the first person to welcome you into this world." Alex looked into Patty's face and saw smiling, soft coffee brown eyes and wished she had remembered this lovely woman. She felt proud that Patty had been such an important part of her life. "How is your Mum?"

"Mum's fine thanks and still blaming me for her loss of figure and obviously not the cakes" She caught Patty's grin and carried on "Would you answer a few questions for me?"

"Just ask, if I feel comfortable about it, I will but we won't know until you ask, so what is it you'd like to know?"

"I'm trying to find out about the abandoned baby from 2003 that was left at the door of the hospital." Alex held her breath, hoping Patty would talk to her.

"After all this time? I thought everyone had forgotten about that by now." Patty was interested now; there was a gleam in her eye that hadn't been there previously. "It was a little girl, just a few weeks old; I still worry to this day about her birth mother, really sad. The baby was bundled up in warm clean blankets and was put somewhere that someone knew she'd be taken care of. There's not much more to tell. I think her birth Mother loved her but couldn't cope, the baby had been well cared for."

"Was it you that found her?" Alex wanted to keep the conversation friendly so asked a few pointless questions. Patty was just getting into her stride and enjoying the chat. Alex started to relax and leant back into the hard plastic chair.

"No, not me, it was one of the regular nurses that found her, can't remember her name but she's moved on now. They did bring the baby to me to be taken care of, poor mite had awful colic and was screaming the place down, throat was red raw but apart from that she was a healthy little girl." Patty looked

74

around "Fancy a coffee? If you want to make them the kettle's over there and I'll just go and sort something out to show you, no milk for me but lots of sugar." With that she disappeared from the room. Alex made the coffees and put them on the desk just as Patty came back and placed a small Polaroid photo on the desk. She picked it up; it was the baby, masses of dark hair snuggled deep into red and yellow blankets inside a crisp box.

"She's lovely."

"She was a screamer, that much I do remember" Patty grinned "I always did have a soft spot for her. She was adopted after we had got her over the colic and after the journalists lost interest, didn't take long."

"Do you know who adopted her?" Alex hadn't meant to be so blunt but felt so comfortable she just couldn't help it; it felt like they had been friends forever.

"Ah, well, that I can't tell you." Patty was sitting there looking out of the window looking as if she was having an inward debate. "But I guess I may know someone who may speak to you but I'll have to check first, it's been a long time maybe there's nothing to keep quiet about anymore but it's not my place to tell." She still looked thoughtful.

They drank their coffee and discussed Alex's parents and Mary and Patty was given a decent dose of the family gossip then they parted like old friends.

Chapter Twenty Seven

Jack remembered well his trips to adjoining towns and the time it took rummaging through the house to find the things he wanted so he could spend more time investigating in the tunnel comfortably. The first thing he packed was the family bible, no one at home would miss it and he wanted to study it more and try to link up more drawings, of course the others that were there could be red herrings but he needed to check, he still needed to know what the tunnel was for and where it led.

That was when it struck him, he could still remember it so vividly the clear sensation, that moment of total clarity that seldom strikes but when it does everything becomes so obvious. He could disappear completely and live in the tunnel, no-one would know except Peter and that was fine because he'd need some help, maybe Peter would join him too at some stage, but ultimately he could get away from his life with these people that called themselves his family but just wanted to control him. It was perfect, he rushed to the phone and called Peter and to this day he still remembered the conversation. Peter's reply was "You're crazy, you can't just disappear, you can't live there."

Jack was completely rational "Peter, you are working, have a great family and your independence. You can do whatever you want with your life. What do I have here?

"It'll get b ….." Peter didn't get to finish.

"It won't get better Pete, I have no independence and they took away from me the one thing I truly cared about." Jack felt a lump rising in his throat and his eyes were only just holding back a flood of bitter tears. Peter could hear it in his voice too. "Okay... Okay. You're right but how do you think you can stay there without being found? It's not far enough away from town."

"They'll find me eventually I'm sure but at least I can have some time away, come with me..." He waited for the reply he knew it was a long shot but it would be great to have someone to share it with.

"I can't Jack. You know I can't."

"Will you help me?"

"Try and stop me."

Jack heard the smile in Peter's voice and felt better about it all, it would work out he just knew it.

The following day he waited until everyone was out and collected up some basic things he may need, blankets, pots, cutlery, matches, basic food and drinks, a portable radio and a few warm clothes. He made three trips to the tunnel with overflowing bags, completely unnoticed. He slept well that night. The following day he went to the bank and drew out his savings and went into Wickston and bought a sleeping bag, hammock, first aid kit and a camping stove amongst many other items. Then another trip to pick up candles, soap, lighters, paraffin and some more paraffin lamps this was a bigger job than he'd anticipated. It took a few days and several trips to collect everything he could think he would need he even remembered toilet paper and that brought on a whole new range of problems.

The last day was dedicated to picking up as many batteries, lighters, food and drinks as he could physically carry and of course a couple of boxes full of Mars Bars which were his biggest weakness. The last thing he did was to write a letter to Peter and he left. That was Friday 23rd July 1965.

Chapter Twenty Eight

Alex was sitting at home feeling lonely and daydreaming about Inspector Matthew Jones sweeping her off her feet and treating her like a princess when the phone rang, it was Patty, she wanted Alex to meet her at 'Heart's' tonight at 7.30pm there was someone she wanted her to meet.

'Heart's' was an up market wine bar where all the young, beautiful, well-heeled people went and Alex was only too pleased to have a reason to go, it was somewhere she considered was out of her league in her normal day to day life, she had been once before for a party but she knew she'd need to raise a mortgage in order to purchase a bottle of wine, she spent two hours getting ready to go, not knowing anything about who she was going to meet but she was going to make the most of it.

She arrived a little early to give herself a chance to relax and enjoy the calm atmosphere, she walked up to the chrome and glass bar and ordered a glass of house red, and perched on the bar stool looking around at the palms and lilies that lined the walls, they had used rows of peace lilies to create the divides between the tables, it was cool, inviting and relaxing. Her mind drifted to a romantic meal with champagne and oysters and Matthew sitting opposite her, eye's sparkling, making her feel incredibly special. She was abruptly brought out of her daydream by Patty's voice "Hey dreamer, you're early" Patty looked gorgeous in a purple outfit with a cream silk scarf. Next to her was a slight woman with perfect blonde hair cut in a soft bob and perfectly manicured nails that perfectly matched her white and pink trouser suit, she looked tiny next to Patty, together they looked a bit like a female Laurel and Hardy but with serious style.

"You look great." Alex said

"You scrub up well too hunny." Patty showed her huge grin "I'd like you to meet Mel; I thought she may be able to help you with your story." When the introductions were all taken care of they were greeted by a waiter who showed them to their table deep amongst the peace lilies. Alex felt a bit nervous, she hadn't expected to eat here and didn't know if she could afford it but if there was a story she knew she had to stay, whatever the cost, luckily she had her credit card with her and she wasn't completely maxed out this month, yet.

They chatted politely about the weather and how beautiful the bar was until the menus arrived, Alex had resolved to not even look at the prices just to order and worry about the cost later, which was what she did, once the salads started arriving and the waiter had moved away from the table Mel looked at Alex and told her story. "Patty told me you were looking for the family who adopted the abandoned baby in connection to some deaths in town; can you keep the family's name out of the papers?"

"I'm not looking for the child" Alex assured her "I'm looking for a link to what's been happening in this town and I just thought the baby might be a part of it, nothing more." Alex was sure now that there was something going on or why would Mel be anxious about anyone knowing about the baby.

"They cannot be named, promise me."

"Of course I won't if that's what you want." She replied honestly.

"Okay, I get the feeling I can trust you and Patty certainly thinks I can, so I'll tell you about Lily, she'll be 12 this year, she's a great kid, she knows she was adopted but doesn't know she was abandoned and that's the way we like to keep it. We worry that at her age it will affect her confidence and make her feel unloved and I can assure you there was never a more loved little girl."

"So she's your daughter?"

"No, no it was my sister that always wanted children but couldn't have any and was over the moon to adopt a baby, especially one so beautiful."

"So everyone's happy now then? So why all of the secrecy for all of these years, it wouldn't have hurt Lily to know when she was younger, she could have dealt with it, kids are resilient that way aren't they?" They started on the food and it was every bit as good as the reputation promised.

"Yes I agree but there was something else too" She stopped and put her fork down to reach for her wine before returning to the conversation, the sharp taste of the wine appeared to spur her on "When they first had Lily they spent a little time away from town with my parents, just until the gossip calmed down, you know how this town is. Well when they bought her back, I suppose it was maybe a little over a year later, there started to be bunches of wild flowers that would turn up on their doorstep."

"Wild flowers? That's nice isn't it?"

"Maybe if they had known where they were coming from it would have been but from time to time they also noticed a woman hanging around by their house, could have been nothing but it unnerved my sister all the same." She stopped as if she had said too much already.

"Did she speak to her?"

"No, but my brother in law Steve followed her a few times and thought he would try to talk to her and see what she wanted, they were scared... it may have been her baby and she'd try to take Lily away. She would always walk away when she saw him and walk around the town, a couple of times he followed her and watched her walk away from the town over the fields but there's only the nature reserve that way so he thought she was just trying to lose him, he let her go."

"So he never spoke to her?" Alex was bemused if it had been her she would have run out and grabbed the woman and demanded to know who she was. She didn't want to interrupt the conversation and say so or she may have made Mel reluctant to talk and for now she was in full flow. They ordered a second bottle of wine whilst still picking at their food and Mel continued.

"Yes he did, one day he turned up at home early and saw her standing under a tree opposite the house holding a small bunch of flowers, he sat in his car and watched her go up to the front door place the flowers down and bow her head as if she was saying a prayer, then she turned and walked back to the tree almost out of sight of the house. He walked up behind her and surprised her, asked who she was and where she was from, she refused to answer any questions even when he threatened her with the police he said it was heart-breaking to see her, she just stood there, tears streaming down her face as she gulped air trying to breath. He softened towards her and invited her into the house but she turned and ran away. He tried to follow her again but she ran across the fields and just disappeared. They never saw her again but the flowers would turn up every year, August 12th without fail, that's how we knew Lily's exact birthday, up until then it was an educated guess." Mel looked almost relieved to have told someone the story, even Patty was surprised, she hadn't known half of the story until tonight.

"They didn't try and catch her bringing flowers on Lily's birthday?" Alex couldn't believe they could let it go there.

"No they didn't, Steve had been disturbed by her reaction when he tried to talk to her previously and I think he felt sorry for her, he said until that day he had never known what it was to hear someone genuinely sob so they decided to leave it alone, she'd never tried to approach Lily, he didn't believe her to be a threat. In fact quite the opposite he wanted to see her again and let her know that Lily was healthy and loved."

"Was there anything about this woman that gave any clues as to what sort of person she was" Alex couldn't see any link between the baby and the bodies; this was a dead end but a pleasant evening all the same. The waiter returned and asked if they would like to order desserts, all of them agreeing that they shouldn't but that wasn't going to stop them, the dessert trolley was rolled towards them and it took them several minutes to choose from the mouth-watering display.

They returned to the conversation, as she was rummaging through her bag Mel added "There wasn't anything really unusual about her, here I have a photo that Steve took from the house one day, it's not great but you can just see her. She was a pleasant looking girl, whenever they saw her she was dressed in jeans and a tatty looking T-shirt, trainers, nothing unusual except a tattoo on her hand, just a design you can't see it on here though."

Alex scrutinized the photo, it was grainy and there wasn't really anything to see except a woman with long dark hair but no real definition. "What was the design like? Did Steve get a good look at it?"

"Yes he said it was loops and looked a bit like a Celtic design with a heart, he had seen something like it once when he was jewellery shopping for Angie's birthday, I think he called it a triquetra but with more loops around it, a more delicate design and it was in two colours, green and red ." Alex went momentarily hot, her skin prickled, that sounded like it was the same design as was on the bracelet that Inspector Jones had sent to her. "Alex, are you okay?"

"Yes sorry, the tattoo might mean something. I won't reveal this in a story but I will need to discuss this with the police, are you ok with that?"

Mel was, which was a relief to Alex. It may be nothing but she would have to pass that information on. Mel had no more information and she began to relax once the story was told, the three ladies settled back and enjoyed the bottle of wine and chatted and laughed, it turned out to be a very pleasant evening.

Chapter Twenty Nine

The first few days in the tunnel were exciting and Jack explored and cleaned and got to know his surroundings, after that he started getting bored and the thought of going home held a certain odd appeal, he couldn't get much reception on his radio unless he went outside but he was worried that he may be discovered if he did, so he would sit by the entrance and have the radio on really quietly, he was missing having someone else around. Instead of running home he decided to make a cover for the entrance, there was plenty of old wood lying around and it was dry and light so it would be easy to push open; he needed a project to keep himself from thinking about being alone. Once that was done he set about moving his things further into the tunnel he wanted to try and see if he could get through the blocked tunnels that he'd found. After a few days he gave up on the one dead end in the tunnel, there was too much stone and he couldn't budge it, he needed heavier tools. He decided to take a break and take a book outside and sit by the well wall and relax, he took his radio with him too. He turned it on and lay back in the grass enjoying the warm sun on his skin, the local station was playing the Beach Boys 'I Get Around' and suddenly Jack found himself starting to relax, he smiled and realised he had done the right thing. He waited for the news report and found he was headline news, he had expected that but he just hoped he wasn't found, he wanted to stay here a while longer yet, he'd go home when he was ready. Over the following couple of weeks his name was mentioned less and less with no sightings for anyone to go on and no-one had found him, he knew soon they would stop looking and he would be old news and finally he started to relax.

He spent some time at the furthest end of the tunnel, here there were steps leading up to a small doorway, Jack was convinced this was the doorway into the library but he couldn't get it open, it was jammed or so it seemed, no keyhole, no obvious hinges he couldn't find a way in. After having a good look round using the bright torch he swapped to the paraffin lamp and his eyes adjusted quickly, he knew he had some rubble to move from the base of the door and he worked at it until his fingers bled with the handling of the ragged stones, several times he had to walk all the way back through the tunnel to get to the well, the last thing he needed was for his hands to get infected. He worked on the door for 3 days but after the first day he used the gardening gloves he had bought with him. He removed all of the stones and placed them at the bottom of the stairs along the tunnel so he wouldn't fall over them and returned to the door, he ran his fingers around the edge of the door and he could have sworn it moved a little or maybe he was just so tired that was what he wanted to believe. He kept working at it for what seemed like hours, he was glad he had eventually thought to bring a bucket of water with him from the well he didn't fancy having to walk about four miles back to the well to clean up, he did curse himself for not thinking to bring some sort of trolley with him to move things easily through the tunnel. He kept moving pushing and pulling the door but nothing happened, he sat down with his back to the door exhausted and his palm came across a stone that felt different to the others, it was smooth with a slight dip in the centre, no bigger than a golf ball, he leant on it with all his weight he heard a click and the door shifted, it had released a clip that was holding the door shut, he pulled the door inwards, the entire door came away from the frame. It was a good job it wasn't a full size door or he would have gone tumbling down the stairs with the weight and this one was heavy enough, he placed it against the wall and light poured in, artificial light, it was coming from a street lamp. The light lit up the room and seemed bright to him after he had been seeing with nothing more than a paraffin lamp for days, he pushed the bookcase to the side, kicked off his shoes and entered the children's reading room, the cartoon faces smiled down at him lit by the street lamp outside and he couldn't help but smile back at them.

He walked into the main room of the library and pulled out the leather librarians chair and just sat there enjoying the luxury of the seat, looking around at the desk there were the date stamps, pens, and some letters that hadn't been posted yet and a large ledger that he knew held the names of people with overdue books his name was in there somewhere, he didn't stay long, he didn't want to be seen but now he could get into the library and had unlimited access to all the books he could possibly read. He looked to his right at the notice board and was shocked to see a poster with his face on it, so they hadn't given up on him yet. He smiled. No-one should be able to see him from outside if he was careful, there were enough bookcases and shadows to hide him, he looked up at the large wall clock it was quarter past three in the morning and nothing moved outside. He let himself into the private room behind the desk; he had never been in there before but hoped there may be something he could eat in there. He was lucky that night, there was a bottle of Coke and half a cheese sandwich. He silently blessed Mrs Sharp for not being hungry that day, there was also a banana on the table, he knew he shouldn't push his luck but he was so hungry it disappeared in two bites.

He went to the public toilet area and had a wash and used the hand soap to wash out his T-shirt it was such a simple pleasure washing in a sink, he felt like he'd been blessed, clean and fresh he returned through the doorway, first pulling the bookcase into place, putting his shoes back on and then dragging the door across and pushing it into the wall until he was satisfied he had heard the click of the door slotting into place. Feeling much better now he returned through the tunnel to the area he was using to live in. He was extremely content that night and slept until the following afternoon.

Chapter Thirty

Inspector Jones was sitting behind his desk lost in thought whilst he waited for his appointment with Alex; she had called him this morning and said it was important. He couldn't wait to see her but she had sounded pure business on the phone. Wanted to see him, said it was important etc. etc. etc. Personally he wasn't bothered about the information, he knew he should be but all he could think about was seeing her; he wanted to see, touch, smell her, he had rarely felt this way about anyone yet he still knew it couldn't work, they would always be at odds with each other, and it still didn't stop him wanting to try.

There was a gentle tap at the door "Come." he abruptly responded having been snapped out of his personal thoughts. Alex walked into his office frowning a little "Sorry Alex, I was miles away."

"Thank you for seeing me so soon Matthew."

He relaxed "And who gave my name away?"

"Mary... my Grandmother, I hear you two know each other." She teased.

"Ah Mary, yes we're old friends." He watched her face carefully, it changed from friendly to business in a heartbeat.

"Seriously, I came to give you some information that you asked for, I hope it helps. The design on the bracelet that you mailed me, I think it's been seen somewhere else" She leant back in the chair and explained the conversation she had with Mel the previous evening and her request for confidentiality.

"So the abandoned baby is a part of this too, looks like I underestimated you Alex."

"So do you have any off the cuff ideas about how they may be linked?"

"Like maybe she was the baby's grandmother... no that can't be right she surely wouldn't have allowed her grandchild to be dumped... sorry... abandoned. Or maybe they're both part of a sect." He smiled at her. "In Charmsbury... Really!"

Alex heard the sarcasm in his voice. "I'm trying to help you, don't ridicule me." She was itching to get out of this room now as she could feel her anger building and she didn't want him to see how much he was winding her up.

"Sorry Alex but it's just a design and they may not have been the same but I will get someone to look into it OK?" He tried to smooth things over now he could see she was reacting badly to his attempt at humour.

"I've already checked it out, it's a design based on a triquetra, there are thousands of tattoo designs along this line on the internet, I couldn't find anything exactly the same though. It's an ancient Celtic symbol believed to be spiritually representing the power of three it's believed to be a magical number and the loops and swirls could represent Balance or Eternity, the heart would obviously mean love."

"Wow you have been busy."

"It's my job Matthew but what I don't know is why they would have it, any ideas? I cannot link it to anything except loosely to druids and spiritual beliefs; it really means nothing to me." She felt relieved now all the information had been shared, she waited for his help.

"No" Was the simple answer that she got and her fury returned.

"Would you tell me if you did know Matthew? Alex didn't wait for an answer, she had suddenly realised how one sided this was all becoming and she stood to leave. He didn't even seem to be listening to her.

Matthew had been sitting studying Alex, getting lost in the soft blonde of her hair and the deep silver grey of her eyes, the curve of her neck. Suddenly he realised she had asked him a question. "Sorry?" But by the time the word was out she was moving away from the desk. "Alex" Too late she had left and he didn't know what had really happened all because he was too busy lusting after her.

Chapter Thirty One

Peter had finally decided that after all these years he could no longer keep going to see Jack, he had been helping him out for fifty years but recently his health had been failing and he could no longer manage the long walks and the dark enclosed areas. He guessed Jack would try to change his mind but this was just the way it had to be now although it would be sad to know this was the last time he would see the tunnel, it had been the biggest adventure of his life and he was glad he had shared it with Jack. He secretly wished he'd been as brave as Jack to live there but his path was to work and have a more normal life, he'd done well in his life he was now a manager at the factory he started work a little over 50 years ago and he had only done that as a favour to his father, strange the way life pans out but it had given him a good life he had met his wife there too, they soon got their own house and mortgage and had three children in quick succession, now they were all grown up and had flown the nest. They rarely kept in touch and by way of thanks life had taken his wife from him quite suddenly, in an accident in her treasured Mini Cooper, within twelve months he was handed the big C. He often wondered if it could have been different if he'd just ran away with Jack and hidden out in the tunnel but then he'd have never met his wife and he couldn't imagine his life without her in it. When he realised that he understood why Jack had to do what he did, how could he live without his Mary.

He knew he'd have to go and see Jack one last time and explain.

The doctors had given him twelve months to live and he needed to get things in order before he could no longer function properly, stage four lung cancer and he'd never smoked, life's a bitch. The chemotherapy had slowed its progress down but he no longer wanted to put himself through that and wanted to spend what time he had left doing all the things he'd been putting off for years for one reason or another.

The first thing was to go and see Jack and explain whilst he still could, they had been friends for too long and had such big adventures together, they were as close if not closer than brothers. He set about packing up a few things for the trip, he would go the next day and he still needed to do his normal shopping for Jack before he went. He was never sure of Jack's reaction if he didn't show up with a box of Mars Bars. He smiled to himself and ran his hand over his now bald head, he needed a hat too.

Chapter Thirty Two

Today was hot, the good weather wouldn't last much longer so he had put his shorts on and sat down leaning his back to the well as he always did on days like these to enjoy some of the sunshine, his body didn't look as good as it used to and he hated old age setting in but the sun still felt good against his skin and made him feel younger and stronger.

Initially he had suffered some boredom and loneliness in the tunnel and a few times had been ready to give it all up and return home with his tail between his legs. But then he had discovered the entrance to the library and had an unlimited access to as many books as he wanted to read and as much knowledge as he wished to soak up and access to a bathroom, he soon found a rhythm to his days. Most days he would sit right here by the well and read, pick some fruit if there was any to be had and do some work on his new home, he was proud of the way it was beginning to feel comfortable. When he was running short on food he would try to disguise himself and take a walk to a town as far away as possible, he thought if he used different towns and villages in rotation he at worst would be considered a returning tourist. It was no problem for him to walk ten or fifteen miles to shop; he loved to walk although he didn't know what he'd do when his money ran out. His daily routine pleased him on the whole and approximately once a week he would visit the library to swap his books and enjoy the luxury of a clean bathroom. On some occasions he had been really lucky to find a bit of fresh milk or fruit in the staff room, he felt bad about taking it but he would feel a lot worse if he didn't, the one thing he couldn't risk was getting ill, which would be worse than getting caught. Once the fresh fruit amongst the brambles was starting to run low he began to teach himself how to grow his own fruit and vegetables, he knew he had to be very careful but he managed to start off a small plot that was partially hidden behind a wall of trees that was enough to feed himself from and it was cheaper and easier than shopping, he had been really pleased when the first tomato or strawberry had ripened, it was a really big achievement for him. The longer he was not discovered the more of a home the tunnel became and he had a small grasp of self-sufficiency, only small because he still needed to shop and use money but it all helped to stretch out his savings.

After three months there seemed to be no more talk of him being missing on the radio or in the newspapers from what he could find out, he got most of his newspapers from the bin in the library, they seemed to stock several of the daily nationals and a local paper that came out weekly. He was grateful that the cleaning in the library wasn't done until the mornings or his access to news and occasional food would have been scuppered.

Around the same time he had a visitor, Peter, Jack looked at his pal in his fashionable clothes and short haircut and thought how different they were, how could they have changed so much in such a short time? Peter came bearing gifts, so many gifts he could hardly carry everything. He had brought food, clothes, a few more tools even cushions, bedding and towels and the best present ever a box of Mars Bars. Peter had stayed for three days funding takeaway food and even a couple of bottles of beer which they walked to collect in the evenings.

That was when it really felt like home. Jack had shown Peter around and taken him to the library, Jack always thought of it as Peter's home too. They worked, laughed, sang, talked and cried together. Their lives were taking very different paths and although it wasn't said they both knew they wouldn't see so much of each other in the future.

The sun was starting to cool a little as it slowly made its descent over the hills Jack got up and went inside to get something to eat. Maybe tonight he would take a walk and treat himself to a beer somewhere, he wanted to walk and he wanted to be alone.

Chapter Thirty Three

She had decided to walk into work today, the story had to be written and although she had the baby information she could not use it, so she needed to go through the archives again and see if there was anything else to find. She had finally realised that talking to Inspector Matthew Jones was a complete waste of her energy; he didn't appear to take her seriously and certainly wasn't forthcoming with any information to help her story. He even had the nerve to accuse her of trying to do a 'Hercule Poirot' as he put it because she wanted a story and was treating the police like grunts that should be doing the groundwork for her. She just knew there was something more to this story and she was even starting to get some great feedback on it, no information but people had emailed her saying they loved her writing and wanting to know what else she would be writing about in the future. The positive feedback had spurred her on and from now on she must work out all of the answers on her own.

She worked in the office most of the day drawing a blank, just a few additional bits of information on the bodies and a missing person story about some rich kid in the 60's but nothing worthy of writing about, so now it looked like she would have to re-hash the information she already had and look for a new slant on the story or drop it completely.

Eventually she decided to leave it for the day and take a walk to her Nan's. It seemed a little cooler out this afternoon; she hoped that meant that this heat wave was burning itself out. She took the short bus ride into Charmsbury and walked along the High Street, she could have gone a couple of stops further on but she needed to pick up some bits and pieces from a local shop and decided to get some flowers for her Nan, it would make a change for her Nan to be spoilt, she was always doing things for other people.

By the time she had picked up her shopping she was in a far better frame of mind although the hope of the heat wave finishing had been damned, it was getting hotter again; Alex could live without this heat. She walked along the High Street and turned up into Clarkes Street and crossed the road to try and get in the shade where it would be cooler, she walked alongside the library and took in the beauty of the old building, something caught her eye and there in the corner of a window was a translucent sticker with a triquetra on it with a heart weaving through it. She stood there just staring at it for a good few minutes, trying to work out what it was doing there and tracing the picture in her mind to see if it really did match. She was sure it did, she found her phone in her bag and went to check it against the email Matthew had sent her. There was no reception, of course, there's never any reception when you needed it she thought but the library would have computers or maybe even Wi-Fi. She quickly took a photo of the sticker and entered the library.

It was cool inside and dark, it took a moment for her eyes to adjust. There was a man sitting behind the desk that was taking no notice of her, after a couple of coughs to attract his attention he finally looked up with no hint of amusement; no they didn't have Wi-Fi but if she had a library card she could use the ancient computer in the corner for up to thirty minutes.

Problem being she hadn't had a library card since she was sixteen and with him being less than helpful she wasn't going to get anywhere here. She asked him about the sticker but he just shrugged and returned to whatever he was trying to do. It looked like she would have to work it out for herself when she got home, maybe the library home page would offer some information. She shrugged and made her way back out into the sunshine.

Finally she arrived at the pretty farmhouse and her Nan was pleased to see her, the endless train of biscuits and cakes came out for the occasion, they chatted about all the gossip she had got and especially about the library, Mary assured her that Sandra the head librarian would be there tomorrow and she may know about the triquetra, but above all Mary seemed more concerned with her not wanting anything further to do with Matthew, Alex was sensing a bit of matchmaking had been going on behind her back. If she was honest she was going to miss having the excuse to see Matthew, his suave good looks and his cheeky slightly lopsided grin anymore but she also didn't want the kind of attention that he had been giving her; that was not a good place to start a relationship.

Chapter Thirty Four

Jack walked out across the nature reserve and away from Charmsbury towards a little village he hadn't visited for over a year, there was a nice little pub in Blunford with a large beer garden and enough tourists to make him inconspicuous and for once he felt like a long cool beer or two.

He ordered his beer and settled into a bench by the side of the river, he watched a couple of families with young children running around chasing a ball and suddenly felt a pang of loneliness, a feeling that he should have had that too but then he had been the one who decided to lock himself away from the world and have an adventure, too late now if it was the wrong decision. If he had been with Mary things would have been so very different, he couldn't believe how he still missed her after all of these years and how restless he was feeling since they had lost Ruby. He took a sip of his beer and relaxed into the bench, this was a good place to be, and he needed the peace.

Over the years Jack had become quite the gardener and handyman he could turn his hand to most things that needed doing or making but he was still struggling to work out the blocked entrance in the tunnel, there was so much to do the time flew by, he had managed to get through the winters by keeping busy, building himself small fires of fallen wood and anything dry that he could find. He had to be careful what he was burning but the tunnel was big enough to disperse most of the smoke. He would also sneak into the library at night when the weather got too bad. One night he got his timing wrong and opened the doorway up and as he stood up, across the library he saw Mrs Sharp locking the door, just leaving the building, either he had got there too early or she had stayed late he couldn't remember anymore but he was convinced she had seen him but she carried on letting herself out and locking the door, if she had seen him she didn't betray him. He hid inside the tunnel again for a while before returning and braving the staff room to get warm by the small three bar fire. The memory was still fresh in his mind, on the table had been a jumper and a flask of coffee, he had put the jumper on to get himself really warm and drank every last drop of that sweet warm liquid, it had been a long time since he had felt so good, and he fell asleep right there and slept for six hours in that warm room, it didn't seem strange to him at all at the time that drinks and clothes were left there. He never took the clothes, just wore them to get really warm and took them off to return to the tunnel, it would have been stupid to steal them and risk giving himself away. Over the years he had wondered if Mrs Sharp had done it on purpose and had somehow known that someone was using the library at night especially when they were cold ones because food and hot drinks were almost always made available, he never saw the flask again but a kettle and a small fridge was installed in the staff room and there was never a shortage of tea, coffee, sugar and fresh milk. He tried not to use too much of anything so it wouldn't be noticed and always left the clothes where he found them until one particularly cold winter, thinking back it must have been a winter in the late 60's around Christmas time and there appeared a wonderful heavy duffel coat with a note pinned to it that simply said. 'Take it if you need it'. He was nervous about taking it and so grateful at the same time, that was when he truly realised the library was the safest place for him to be. He always wondered if Mrs Sharp knew it was him or not, if she did she never tried to trap him, she was just kind, he'd wished he could tell her just how much that had meant to him through those cold lonely winters, in return he left her a hand drawn picture of his favourite design and left it in the same place that she had left the coat for him, it was the first Christmas present he had given to anyone for years. Peter would turn up occasionally with provisions too and when he did it was wonderful to have the company and the fresh food, then in May of 1969 Peter turned up with someone else in tow, the shock of Peter giving this place away to someone else was so much of a shock that Jack hid himself away in one of the rooms hoping they would just go away, he stayed there for an hour before rationalizing why Peter would do this; he had realised he had turned into a hermit, he had settled into a life of being alone and never questioned it and now he needed to talk himself around. Eventually he decided he was being stupid because there must be a really good reason that Peter would bring someone to his home but he felt nervous and frightened, he knew he had to overcome these feelings and face the world head on.

It was a man around the same age as they had been when they found the tunnel. He had long lank brown hair and looked like he needed a bath; he had been living rough in Sunderland after having a huge row with his family which resulted in them throwing him out. He looked terrible and smelt worse but it turned out he had a great sense of humour. Jack never found out what the row had been about or why he didn't want to return to his family it was never spoken about, Jack wasn't a councillor he couldn't even sort his own life out what chance did he have trying to sort someone else's out. Jerry had moved into the tunnel there and then, the only proviso was for him to clean himself up. Peter had met Jerry when he went out on business one day and they had got talking and got to know one another quite well over the space of six months and Peter had thought that Jack would like Jerry, they might get on well and they could help each other out as it didn't look like Jack would be leaving the tunnel any time soon. Peter had stayed just overnight and gone home again leaving Jack and Jerry to work things out. His parting gift had been a cheeky two boxes of Mars Bars so they didn't have to share. Peter had left with a smile on his face, he thought it would turn out fine.

After the initial feeling of being put upon by Peter and a little resentment Jack had liked Jerry he was an easy guy to get along with and having a companion in the tunnel made life much more pleasant; there was plenty of space so they didn't have to see too much of each other and they respected each other's privacy but it was good having someone else to share the load. Jerry had very little money and few possessions but turned out to be very skilled in the garden and he could make almost anything that they needed, he was good with his hands and had a real talent as a carpenter.

Jack didn't take Jerry into the library; he wanted to keep that as his little secret pleasure for as long as he could.

Jack drained his glass and feeling more relaxed than he had in quite a while he started to make his way home, the cool evening air making him feel good to be alive.

Chapter Thirty Five

She'd had two phone calls this morning and Mary was beginning to wonder why Alex and Matthew wouldn't just give it a try, they had both called her complaining about the other but obviously both were too stubborn to contact the other directly. Mary wondered why they were making it so complicated and she told them both to grow up and get on with it. She would love to see them together she was sure they would make a good couple but she refused to interfere, she knew how things ended when other people got involved. She gazed out of her farmhouse window beyond the little garden that could use a little bit of attention but was still pretty; she thought she would get around to it later. Her gaze took her over the fields, would she have still had this view if she had been with Jack or would she have moved away and had a very different life? She would never know. She snapped out of that line of thought knowing it would only make her maudlin for the rest of the day.

She picked up her door keys from the side table, and dropped them in her bag, checked her purse was in there and closed the door behind her, she had decided she needed a walk, maybe she could pick up a couple of things she needed en route but she really needed some fresh air. She headed towards town.

On the road into town she noticed a new coffee shop the 'Red Bean', she thought it a strange location on the edge of the town centre but maybe the rent was cheaper here, the prices in the centre of town had risen considerably over the last few years. She rarely walked into town; the car was more convenient otherwise she may have spotted the coffee shop sooner. She decided to give it a try and she loved good coffee and the sign outside promised her the best coffee money could buy. Inside it was cool and fitted out in old fashioned wooden panelling and rustic furniture and lots of plants. She ordered herself a Macchiato; she thought it sounded extravagant enough to match her surroundings. Charmsbury was definitely going up market; she really was enjoying all the changes going on around the town. New shops, the bistro, this new coffee shop and all the money the council were spending on doing up the park and it was looking lovely with all the new plants and the bright colours that the benches, play area and fences were being painted. She was pleased she still lived here with all of its bitter sweet memories and even the macchiato lived up to expectations.

As she got ready to leave she glanced over to a corner table, which she couldn't see when she was seated and noticed a man sitting with his coffee, deep in thought writing a letter, he would glance up from time to time and stare into space as if looking for inspiration and then having found it he would immediately return to scratching away at the paper. Unusually he was using a fountain pen, Mary hadn't seen anyone write with one of those for many years. He was tall and slim, quite attractive in a worn out kind of way, he seemed vaguely familiar to Mary but she couldn't quite put her finger on who he was. The look of him took her back to when she was a girl but she couldn't quite put her finger on the memory, maybe he just looked like someone she once knew. She picked up her bag, gave the man one last glance but he was still engrossed in his letter writing and left the 'Red Bean'.

She wandered around the town for a while pausing to look in some of the fashionable shop windows. She continued on to the supermarket to do her bit of shopping and as she walked past the library she saw Alex inside, she popped in to see what she was up to.

Chapter Thirty Six

Mrs Eva Sharp the old librarian had been Sandra's Mother in Law. Sandra was only too pleased to talk about her with Alex.

"Eva had been the librarian here for close on forty years before I took over the position." Sandra said "and when she was here you would never have had the problem you encountered yesterday, for which I apologise."

"It wasn't really a problem, I just wanted to know about the significance of the sticker in the window, I've been seeing the design a lot recently and can't seem to find out what it means, and I was hoping you could help." Mentally Alex crossed her fingers.

"Oh that old sticker has been in the window for at least twenty five years and Eva put it there, I have no idea what its significance is." Sandra said "I have just left it there because she was sentimental about it, then I just forgot it was there, so there it's stayed for all these years."

"So, no ideas about it or where it may have come from?"

"No but I'll ask my husband tonight for you, she may have said something to him about it, I don't know."

"What was Eva like? I'm sure I must have met her when I was very young but I'm afraid I don't really remember her."

"Some people thought that Eva was an old battle axe and as tough as old boot leather but the truth is that she was a woman who didn't suffer fools gladly but had a heart of gold and would help anyone in need. She was adored by all of her family and is still greatly missed, she passed away 15 years previously and in the end she had suffered with Alzheimer's a truly sad way to end her life, a shell of the woman she once was." Sandra seemed pleased that someone besides the family remembered Eva and seemed to enjoy talking about her. "She had never wanted to leave the library and always said she had to stay because the library held too many secrets and its fair share of ghosts."

"What did she mean by that?"

"I don't know, nothing's happened here whilst I've been in charge or at least I haven't seen any ghosts and I certainly don't think it's haunted."

"But what made her think it was? It seems like an odd thing to think."

"She used to say things would get moved around and regularly she would run out of milk even though she knew she'd only just bought a bottle or carton. In the winter she would swear that someone or something had been sleeping in the staff room."

"Hello you two, gossiping again Sandra?" Mary smiled.

"Hi Nan, I'm trying to get some background on Mrs Eva Sharp, what are you doing here?"

"Just saw you two gossiping so I thought I'd come and join in."

"What do you say Mary? Think this place is haunted?" Sandra asked.

"Haunted! Oh Alex what are you talking about ghosts for, is this a new assignment?" Mary laughed.

Mary and Sandra started chatting about the past and people Alex didn't know. They were both in their element chatting about how things had been and reliving their youth. Sandra apparently saw talking as an Olympic sport and was well in training, there was little if any useful gossip for Alex but she listened in just the same, apparently Eva had been a walking, talking encyclopaedia on all things to do with the library building and its inhabitants over the years but now she was gone if anyone wanted to know something they had to trawl through the history books. Alex was a little put out that her Nan had interrupted her conversation and had heard enough banal town gossip and so made her excuses to leave, ensuring that Sandra would indeed ask her husband if he knew anything, she would have to come back another day. Ghosts and secrets sounded interesting.

Chapter Thirty Seven

Dave went out early to collect the local papers, which was a relief to Jack, he'd been walking too much recently and was glad of the excuse to sit back and read the newspapers without having to have the exercise. He picked up the Daily News first and skipped through it to see if there was another story but he was relieved to discover nothing about Ruby in this edition, finally the reporter must have run out of steam, he relaxed and went back to the beginning and enjoyed reading the local tittle tattle. His attention then turned to the Charmsbury Gazette the local weekly paper, he knew the story would be here and it was but only a re-run of the story that had been in the Daily News, so now he hoped everything could go back to normal, no new info and the story had passed. He noticed an article on page seventeen by 'Alexandra Price' but that was a write up of a local church fete that had happened two days previously and managed to raise almost four thousand pounds for good causes. This made him smile, Alexandra had totally run out of storylines and had been relegated to church fetes, how his fortunes had turned around.

Now he felt safe to relax and he could start looking forward to Peter's visit, it was normally around this time that he would appear and stay for a short while, he knew Peter hadn't been well the previous time he visited and was hoping that he would be back to his old self this year and visit as usual. They usually had a lot of fun when they got together, they normally went out of town for a day or two, then Peter would stay with Jack for a few more days, it was like they relived their childhood whenever they had the chance to get together. Jack needed this visit too he was all too aware that he was getting restless, this happened every so often and he just had to ride the feeling out. As much as he wanted to leave here it was balanced out by how much he wanted to stay and in all honesty he didn't know what he'd do with himself if he did leave. He and Peter had built this up so how could he walk away now? He hated the confusion and indecision but it would pass, it always did.

He remembered that after Jerry had moved into the tunnel life on the whole had got much easier, Jerry wasn't worried about going into the surrounding towns and villages as he wasn't known in the area so on market days he would sometimes go into town and sell some of the small carvings he'd done to fill his time. The tourists seemed to like them, a touch of local art to take home with them as a reminder of their holidays, they always sold well and it gave him money to buy fresh produce that he would always bring back to the tunnel and share with Jack. Jerry even constructed a small outhouse hidden by a patch of trees so at least they would have a little privacy and it was far more comfortable than a hole in the ground, although cleaning it was no pleasure. It marked an evolution in the history of the tunnel and over the following ten years another seven people joined them. It was always people that had been introduced by Peter because he had met them when they were down on their luck and he felt that they needed a fresh start. If Peter liked them then Jack always let them stay and most of the time they were an asset to the community. There was only one rule, Jack still kept the library to himself, and no-one went near the doorway unless they were invited to.

Having more people living with him meant that it wasn't always down to him to do everything, it took him some time to get used to having other people around but he slowly began to realise that it made life much easier for him, it took him much longer to trust them but it turned out that the majority of them genuinely wanted a new start in life, just a chance to prove themselves worthwhile. He suddenly found he had spare time now he was no longer responsible for everything, they would take it in turns cooking and cleaning and making the tunnel feel more pleasant. There had been a woman called Owl, he never discovered her real name but she would sit up all night, every night making rugs for the floors and colourful drapes for chairs. She would go into one or two of the towns and pick up old clothes from charity shops, the ones that even they didn't want and make them into all sorts of things the biggest hit was her cushions, there wasn't much comfort in the tunnel until she arrived and she made sure everyone got pillows and mats. What a blessing she had been but she had left them in 1979 when Steve had died; his was the first death in the tunnel that they had to deal with. Steve and Owl had got quite close and she hadn't coped well. Steve's death had been completely natural he just didn't wake up one morning and Owl went off the rails, everyone rallied round to try and help her but she didn't want to be helped. She decided to leave and make her own way and she took the body into Charmsbury close to the river with the help of a couple of the guys and stayed with it until it had been found, then she took off and Jack had never heard from her again. No one ever forgot the lady who made their pillows but everyone who had met her missed her terribly.

Steve's death had been difficult on them all, they didn't know what to do, it had never happened before. They couldn't bring themselves to dig a hole and bury him, someone out in the real world would be missing him; a mother, brother maybe even a wife at least if he was taken back into town there was a chance that his family and friends would at least be able to mourn him, rather than endlessly not knowing what happened to him and always wondering where he was. It seemed the best thing they could do for everybody involved.

Chapter Thirty Eight

Alex was yet again struggling with this story, she'd now found the design three times in three seemingly unlinked places but couldn't manage to put them together. What did it mean? The reference to ghosts and secrets was still playing on her mind too, just her luck that Eva had taken that information to the grave with her. She decided to look into the history of the library, it seemed that Eva loved that place so much, at least she could find out more about her town if nothing else. She made herself a sandwich and poured a glass of wine then half-heartedly she tapped away at the search engine online and discovered that there was a lot more history in her home town than she thought. Where the library was had once been a manor house or a part of one and had quite an interesting history.

The complete building had been a very grand Elizabethan stone built manor house, built in 1597 with other wings completed around 1600, it was set in its own beautiful landscaped gardens and had its own small chapel. It was owned by a local family called Heatheridge for many generations. Edward Heatheridge had made his fortune in law and become mayor of Charmsbury and the surrounding areas. He was very much in love with a young woman named Charlotte and to show his admiration for her he had Heatheridge manor built including the chapel as he was a catholic and liked to practice his religion which was difficult in that period of history and it is believed that he had his own Jesuit priest at the manor, who had been trained in Rome. Edward wooed Charlotte and eventually she agreed to marry him and from that day the manor house stayed in the family for many generations. There was lots of gossip about the family over the years and by 1863 the building needed some serious renovation and extortionate amounts of money spent on it which the family no longer had. The youngest daughter of the family it seemed hated the family home and believed that she had heard voices and seen people moving around the house, she would get so hysterical with fear that the doctor was a regular caller at the house. Eventually the family decided to move to London citing the reason for their move that the manor was haunted by malicious spirits that were out to harm the family. They never returned to the manor and it seemed that no-one else was interested in buying and restoring it, slowly it crumbled to the ground reclaimed largely by nature.

By the 1920's the majority of the building was deemed too dangerous to leave standing and the demolition began, there was one wing and the kitchen area that were still in relatively good condition and builders went in to make what could be saved safe and turn it into a building in its own right. The larger part of the building became the Town Hall and the kitchen area housed the library, the landscaped gardens and remaining land was sold off to developers in lots which created enough money to be able to refurbish the two remaining buildings. The ghosts forgotten in a more enlightened era.

It had stayed this way to the present day although soon the library would be moved to new premises and there was no news about what the old building would be used for.

Alex wondered if it had been haunted although she thought herself far too sensible to believe in such things so thought there must have been more to it, it had been such a beautiful building that she thought it more likely that the family could no longer afford the upkeep of the house and used the daughters fear as an excuse to move away, although no one else had been interested in taking on the house and it was such a stately building, maybe there was something to the ghost story.

Chapter Thirty Nine

Peter drove his car out to the nature reserve and parked up, just a short walk to the tunnel. His intention was to leave the letter he had written to Jack with one of the other members of the community then drive home. He had also slid a thousand pounds into the envelope along with the heartfelt letter, he couldn't face Jack he knew he would take the news badly and he didn't need the upset, he was struggling with his diagnosis himself and knew Jack would be shattered. He hoped the money would encourage Jack to find his way to a more comfortable way of life. As he walked across the wasteland the first person he encountered was Jack, 'sod's law' he thought, he put a smile on his face and walked towards him.

"Hello old friend" Jack said, smiling "Am I glad to see you".

"Hi Jack, it's good to be back" and he realised as he said it he really meant it, how could he have ever thought he could come here and not stayed and discussed things with Jack.

"Come in, come in, there are so many people who will be pleased to see you."

They walked past the bushes and descended into the tunnel, everyone he encountered as he moved through the tunnel smiled, hugged him and patted him on the back, he felt like he'd come home. He began to wonder why he would have ever thought he could avoid the place or why he would even want to.

They walked for a while until they reached the kitchen area which was cool and comfortable; they sat down and had a cup of coffee. At that moment Peter knew he would have to come clean and tell Jack everything. He looked around at the comfortable eating area with its wall art and makeshift seating and was still unable to take in that all of this had worked out so well for so many people. A tear rolled down his face.

"What's wrong Peter?" Jack was immediately concerned, he'd never seen Peter like this, Peter was always in control and taking care of people.

Peter couldn't say anything for a minute he just handed the letter to Jack and looked away as if something really interesting was happening on the mat at his feet, he couldn't look Jack in the eye.

Jack looked at the envelope "What's going on Pete? Talk to me. Please." He placed the envelope on the table and waited.

"Oh Jack, I don't know where to start." Silence ensued and then suddenly it was as if the flood gates had opened "You know I've been ill, it's cancer Jack, they've given me twelve months if I'm lucky, I'm scared, I don't know what to do" He told Jack everything he knew about his illness, about his decision to not go ahead with the treatment and what he wanted to achieve before his time was up. Jack was stunned and hugged his friend like he never wanted to let go, they talked and cried together for hours and Peter answered all of his questions as well as he could but Jack couldn't take it in, it was too much. Jack wanted him to stay with the community and be loved and cared for amongst the people who loved him.

Peter wanted to stay more than anything in the world, he wanted the warmth of people who he knew cared about him but he had so much to take care of and he needed to do it whilst he still could, he was already aware of any exertion taking its toll and he was slowing down and sleeping much more than he used to. He couldn't stay even though it was the only thing he really wanted to do.

Chapter Forty

Alex woke up to three messages waiting for her on her mobile and before she even opened them she had a feeling that this was going to be a good day.

She went to the kitchen and filled the percolator and whilst it was gurgling away and producing the most wonderful aroma she opened the first of the emails. This one was from Sandra informing her that her husband Tony would be at home all day and would be more than happy to have a chat with her about his Mum, her address was at the bottom of the email. Alex thought it was funny the way you could tell someone's age by the way they wrote an email. No abbreviations, no text talk and paragraphs set out precisely usually meant the author was at least 50 years old. If it was from anyone below the age of twenty five you always had to insert all the vowels in the correct place to try and make any sense out of it and then it didn't always work out so well. Sandra's email had been totally old school and punctuation perfect.

So with her morning now organized she poured herself a steaming hot mug of coffee and opened the next email, sent from another string of numbers and no name, it could be spam or it could be her helper the perfect stranger as she had started to think of him or maybe her. She smiled and when the email had loaded all it said was 'Good story. You're getting warmer." That implied all her guesswork was right and there was more to find. She thought it may be time to get the techies at the paper involved to try and find out just who these emails and tweets belonged to; obviously it was someone who was keeping an eye on her. She found this reassuring maybe this story would be a good one if she could stay on track.

She was saving the third email until last, it could be good or bad and she was opting for the latter even though it made her smile just seeing the name. She wondered if Inspector Jones knew she was waking up with him albeit electronically. She took a moment to check her Twitter feed but it was full of cute cats and some news about a dust storm over Dallas, nothing of the slightest bit of interest to her so she went back to her final email of the morning.

She was stunned this one had come out of the blue, Matthew was apologising for being an idiot and not taking her work seriously and not taking her seriously but he put it down to liking her too much. He was offering to take her out for dinner this evening at 'Hearts'. Wow she really hadn't seen this coming and everything she was holding against him melted away in an instant, this was already turning into an awesome day, well things really did happen in threes. She emailed him back and graciously accepted his offer, her stomach immediately started feeling like there were a million butterflies fluttering around trying to get out. Now she would need to go shopping after she had seen Tony and treat herself to a new dress, a haircut and just maybe a pampering session at the local beauticians. She thought he was worth it.

Chapter Forty One

Jack was hurting and he didn't know what to do about Peter, he was distraught and he didn't know what he could do for his friend. If Peter had given up on treatment then he should stay with the community, they could take care of him every bit as well as the treatment he would get if he stayed at home with just a carer to look after him and then eventually a hospice where he would just wait to die. He must try and talk him into having the treatment that might prolong his life or was that just him being selfish, he was really confused, he was lucky enough not to have had to deal with anything like this before and didn't know what the options were. Everyone at the community loved Peter and would do anything for him, he had changed the lives of everyone who was here, without him half of them could be dead by now, and they all owed him a great debt of kindness.

Jack knew he would have to go and see him and attempt to talk him around, Peter had stayed in a hotel in Charmsbury the previous night, he'd said he was too emotional to stay with Jack and it was too late to drive home, he needed to be alone. He would be back when he had relaxed and calmed down but Jack couldn't wait he didn't want to think of Peter on his own and trying to shoulder this alone. It was time for Jack to step up to the mark after all that Peter had done for him. It was the very least he could do and he needed to understand Peter's choices, the previous day had been a blur of emotion and now he had calmed down a little he had to try and understand.

He looked down at the envelope Peter had left for him and decided now was not the time to open it, it would keep, after what they had discussed nothing could be more important than going to see his friend. He put it by the side of his bed, got changed into the best clothes he owned and left to walk into town.

All thought of anyone seeing him had gone out of his mind, he no longer cared all he needed was to see his friend. He knew that Peter would have checked into the Duke on the High Street. He walked not noticing what was around him, long determined strides and a head full of confusion; he didn't need to think, he knew where he was going. The Duke was a place that had been a hotel when he was a child and it was where Peter used to stay with his parents on family holidays, as boys they had hung around the hotel often talking and laughing, it was where he first took Mary to meet Peter all those years ago.

He walked in through the old heavy wooden doors and across the black and white tiled floor to the reception desk; it was cool inside and smelt faintly of disinfectant. There was nothing modern or fancy about this hotel anymore in fact it was just the same as he remembered it, even the colour of the walls were the same, it just looked older and very tired. The receptionist looked like she had been there as long as the building, she was an elderly lady with dyed blonde hair and too much make-up but at least she was smiling.

"Hello I'm looking for Mr Peter Jacobs, could you tell me his room number please?"

"I'm sorry my love Mr Jacobs checked out early this morning." She smiled at Jack.

"Do you know where he went or might he have left a note for me?" Jack mentally crossed his fingers because if he hadn't left a note Jack had little to no chance of finding him.

"No, he didn't leave nothing here, he did mention something about having to see somebody but I didn't take much notice, people come and go all the time in this business." She gave a little laugh at her own joke and went back to tapping on a computer. Jack felt helpless, how was he meant to find Peter now, he had no idea where he could have gone. He just stood at the counter not knowing which way to turn. "Are you okay?" The receptionist's voice cut through his thoughts. "You look a bit pale, can I get you a drink?"

"No thank you, I'll check later to see if he comes back."

"No point my love, he was leaving in his car said he had a long trip ahead, don't expect to see him back here today or else why would he have checked out?"

"Yes, yes you're right, I wasn't thinking, thank you for your help." Jack turned and shuffled out of the hotel, now he was really worried about Peter but he'd just have to wait until he decided to come back in his own time.

Chapter Forty Two

Alex got her things together and went to the address on Sandra's email. She drove up to the house, a nice semi-detached suburban house with a well-kept front garden full of colour and a crazy paved path leading to the front door. Before she got out of her little car she thought she should ring Charlie and let him know what she was up to, she wished she hadn't. Charlie told her to get back to the office and do the jobs that were waiting for her, as she'd already wasted enough time on this story with only one good article to show for it, she begged him to let her carry on but his mind was made up and she should get back to work. She didn't know what to do next and she felt a little guilty; she was here now and had planned to go shopping this afternoon not giving a thought about what anyone at the office may think. Charlie wanted her back and she would go after she had spoken to Tony, Charlie could only shout at her once regardless of what time she got into the office, she would take her chances.

She walked along the crazy paving and up to the door still musing over the reception she would get when she got back into work, it was making her feel a little nervous, maybe it was just that she felt guilty going against Charlie after he had been so good to her but she needed to hear what Tony might have to say. Feeling a little more resolved to her fate she tapped on the door, nothing, she knocked again and harder this time and

125

waited. She heard the sound of the lock giving up its work and a man's voice "Sorry, won't be a minute" came from the other side of the wood. Finally the door swung open and Tony looked up at her from his wheelchair. "Sorry love, it's a bugger opening the door in this chair, sorry, you must be Alex, come in, come in" He beamed at her and she couldn't help but return the warm smile.

"Hello Tony, may I call you Tony?"

"Well it's my name and we don't stand on ceremony here girl, obviously" He grinned and glanced at his useless legs. "Can I get you a drink?"

Just a juice if you have it please, I don't want to put you to any trouble though."

"It's a rare treat for me to have visitors Alex, it's no trouble at all" He disappeared into the next room and a few minutes later appeared with juice and cake and an ashtray. "Don't mind if I smoke do you?"

"Of course not, I may just join you."

They got themselves settled in the beautifully decorated lounge, plush armchairs and lots of soft cushions in all shades of reds and terracotta, there'd been a lot of care put into this room, not too many ornaments or photographs but the room was incredibly comfortable. "So you want to know about my Mum and her work Sandra tells me."

Alex explained everything she knew about Eva and about the sticker in the library window and how she thought it all related to the body that had been found in the park. Tony listened without interruption until she had finished her tale "Well, do you think my Mum was mixed up in all this?"

"No, I just think she may have held the clue to unravel the story, it was Eva who put that sticker on the library window so I assume she knew what it meant, I can't find any link to it.

126

Sandra thought you may be able to share some of your Mum's stories that might shed some light on it."

"I don't know anything about a sticker but she told me many stories of strange things that happened at the library. I think she knew more than she told me too."

"What makes you say that?" Alex took a drink of her juice, eyeing the cake, which hadn't been offered yet.

He wheeled his chair over to an old fashioned roll top writing desk and pulled out a handful of exercise books, the kind that Alex had used at school.

"After she died I found these in the secret compartment of the writing desk, these desks are brilliant for hiding things, there are always hidden drawers and secret panels, the desk used to be in her room and held all her personal paperwork which we had to go through after she died." He proudly held the books out to Alex. "Took me ages to work out all the secret drawers in this one" He grinned.

"What's in them?" Alex reached out to accept the books.

"Why don't you read them and find out."

"I have to get back to work I don't have time to read them now, can't you give me a clue."

"No I meant you could take them with you and read them at leisure, it might make some sense to you, and there are some great stories in there, lots of history too."

"You really wouldn't mind me taking them." Alex was amazed with his kindness.

"No, you just bring them back when you're done with them, I'd like to pass them on through the family one day but if they might help you then she would have wanted you to read them." He paused "Before you go you must help me eat this cake though." They both laughed and a friendship was born.

They chatted for a while about Eva and her family and work but Tony wouldn't give any clues to the books contents he wanted her to read it for herself.

Alex was sorry to leave but promised to visit again soon and headed off to work to face the wrath of Charlie.

Chapter Forty Three

He saw a café up ahead it was one of those big chains so no-one would take a blind bit of notice of him, he needed to stop and think and that seemed like as good a place as any, surely he could work out where Peter might be headed. That was when he realised he'd isolated himself so much that he didn't know much about Peter's life away from Charmsbury apart from what they'd discussed, it took a minute for the penny to drop that he'd known this man almost all of his life and considered him a best friend and now when Peter needed him he didn't know where to begin to help his friend. He stopped at the café and got a hot cup of tea and sat at a table outside, as he started drinking he realised he had the beginnings of a headache, a slow dull thud at the front of his head. He should start on his way home to see if any of the others had spoken with Peter or may have any clues as to where he might have gone. With every minute that passed he could feel his headache increasing in intensity, he rubbed his temples then ran a hand through his thick white hair, he never had been able to handle stress very well, he usually avoided it by running away at least that was what Peter would have said. He drained the remainder of the warm sweet liquid and started walking towards home. The view was lost on him today he just put his head down, deep in thought and kept walking; all he wanted to do was to get home.

By the time he returned most of the others were there but no-one seemed to have any information to share with him and some of them hadn't even seen Peter on this visit. Jack was close to giving up, his head was pounding now and all he wanted was some peace and quiet, he reached his room and with great relief lay down on his bed and closed his eyes, he wanted to rest just for a short while.

When he opened his eyes again he gingerly moved his head and it felt as though the headache had subsided and thankfully there was little pain. He felt like he'd been asleep for maybe an hour but he couldn't see the clock from where he was lying so he reached out to turn the clock around to face him, as it turned he heard something fall to the floor. He noted the glowing red digits 9:30pm, he'd slept for over six hours. As he reached down for what had dropped on the floor his fingers came into contact with the envelope he'd put on the table that morning. He reached out for the lamp and pressed the switch and sat up, just maybe Peter had said where he was going in the letter or at least left a clue, his head had hurt so much when he got back he'd forgotten about the envelope.

He leant back against his cushions and pillows, which Peter had bought for him years ago, and peeled open the envelope. The first thing his fingers encountered was a wad of twenty pound notes; Jack had no idea why Peter would be giving him so much money. As he pulled the notes out several sheets of writing paper came out with them. He placed the money and the envelope to one side and turned his attention to the letter, Peter's neat small handwriting filled up both sides of four pages of the writing paper. The first page was to explain to Jack what was wrong with him and all of the treatment he had gone through and why he didn't want to go through any more of it, all the things they had discussed, then it drifted into the memories Peter had held so dear over the years. As Jack read the tears flowed freely down his face and Peter's explanation of his illness stung Jack as he hadn't known the problem had existed before yesterday and didn't realise what his friend had been through. He felt angry at himself for not being there for his friend, then he felt angry because Peter hadn't allowed him to know and to care for him; he should have shared the agony as they had always shared the joys.

He read on and found many wonderful memories in Peter's words but there were no explanations or hints of where he might have gone and only then did Jack realise how little he had really shared with Peter, yes he had always known him as a friend who had always been there for him and he knew about his work and his wife, he had attended the wedding but he didn't know the details of his life, only the snapshots he had shared when they had a day or two together. Jack didn't know what to do, he felt like he'd let his friend down and from the tone of his letter he thought he may never see him again. Jack realised he'd been a selfish fool and he had to find a way to put things right.

The letter went on to say that Peter had never blamed him for the way things had turned out over the Jonathon incident and he was sorry that Jack had never found a way to heal and to love again, as he had only ever loved one woman Peter felt it would be right to find out what had happened to her to put Jack's mind at rest. The next paragraph blindsided Jack; Peter had written

> *'Jack I want you to know that Mary is well and still lives in Charmsbury, she married and had a family but her husband died a few years ago, for your own sanity Jack for God's sake go and see her, even if you only do it for me, think of it as my last wish.'*

That was followed by her address.

In that moment Jack managed to laugh and cry, happiness and anger at the same time his emotions just folded in on him, his hands shook and he shivered hot and cold. Mary was alive and well, he glanced up at the perfume bottle on his bookshelf "Thank you Peter" he whispered hoping somewhere Peter would sense his thanks. Now he needed to find his friend and thank him properly.

Chapter Forty Four

She stood in front of the mirror checking every last detail. She'd had no chance to go shopping that afternoon and when she'd finally got to the office, Charlie had done the equivalent of grounding her. She had been given a file on local shop openings and closings over the past two years and was told to come up with a story, she hadn't moved from her desk for over four hours, she had struggled to find a story amongst the figures laid out in front of her especially as her mind was on the forthcoming evening. Eventually she had managed to cobble a story of sorts together and Charlie had nodded and told her to go home and not to be late tomorrow.

She'd gone straight home and frantically started pulling clothes out of the wardrobe trying to mix and match the perfect outfit, finally after narrowing it down to three she sank into a hot bath full of sweet smelling oils and pampered herself. As if it knew the importance of this evening her hair behaved beautifully as she styled it into a sleek bob and her make up went on perfectly first time. She finally chose a fitted black dress with delicate plum coloured lace trimming around the shoulders. As she inspected herself in the mirror she was happy with what she saw looking back at her.

There was a knock at the door, Alex approached slowly, it felt like butterflies were beating their wings in a frenzy in her stomach and she couldn't remember the last time she had felt this way about anyone. She opened the door and for a moment that seemed to last for minutes they stood there admiring each other, no words were needed there was an electricity that flowed between them and then the spell was broken as he handed her a bunch of white roses and smiled.

"You look beautiful." He breathed.

"Thank you Matt, come in whilst I find a vase for these, they're beautiful. Did you have inside information on my favourite flowers?" She smiled at him, she knew he had and he just nodded, she knew her Nan would have a hand in this somewhere. As he brushed past her into the house she could smell that expensive cologne again and she gave an involuntary shiver, he looked deliciously good too in a beautiful light grey suit it took all of her self-control to keep her hands off him. She closed the door and walked past him to lead the way to the kitchen hoping she was getting some admiring glances too. Twenty minutes later they were still in her kitchen talking and drinking wine, they were both starting to relax with each other. She couldn't believe how well they were getting along after all the bickering of previous meetings. Finally they left and went to Hearts for dinner, it was perfect, the whole evening was fun and she couldn't remember when she had laughed so much. They'd both managed to avoid discussing their work so conversation was easy and Matthew was the perfect gentleman.

He drove her home, walked her to the door, leaned in close and gently took her face in his hands and kissed her, she had been waiting all evening for the first kiss and it did not disappoint. Then he did it again and she responded, it soon built up into a deep lingering kiss and neither one of them wanted to break the spell. He looked into her eyes, smiled and turned around and left her wanting more.

Chapter Forty Five

She had managed to get into work on time the next morning and not even Charlie could wipe the smile off her face, she decided to use the time to do some more background on the library and to start reading Eva's notebooks that Tony had given to her just so long as Charlie didn't come up with another pointless story to keep her occupied.

Eva's handwriting was a beautiful script, the letters perfectly upright and evenly spaced she obviously had taken a huge pride in her writing and it was easy to read. The first book was mainly the history of the building and aside from a few minor points it was what Alex had found out online, nothing out of the ordinary there and no surprises. The second book started to bring things more up to date, why the decision was made to save the buildings and use them for the good of the town, the then Mayor a Mr Briggs had always hankered after the building even in its rundown state, he didn't have the funds himself but he was in the position as Mayor to push the idea of the town claiming it for their own and spending their budget on doing it up and to save it for the future. There's no doubt it is a beautiful building and even if he did it for personal reasons he certainly did the town a big favour. Eva had written a foot note saying that the building was a Catholic building. Alex didn't know what the reference meant but she was sure she could work it out as she read more.

The third book was dated on the front 1961 and was written more as a journal rather than a history book, it described things she was doing at work and gave an insight into the world of the librarian in that era. She had catalogued all of the library's books by hand, no computers, they only had them in the city and according to Eva she didn't want any of those new-fangled machines in her library the card index system would do her fine. Alex was beginning to like Eva she seemed to be a matter of fact, take no messing kind of woman; she certainly took a pride in her library. It also mentioned a few of the people that used the library and some funny anecdotes' about them. It helped her form a picture of the woman and the work but there wasn't much more to be gleaned from this notebook. She moved on to the next.

"Alex aren't you going to lunch today" It was Fiona, the girl in the next office. "Whatever you're working on must be good we've not heard a peep out of you all morning. A few of us are going for coffee if you want to join us?"

"Can I take a rain check Fi? I've got to catch up on some stuff, maybe tomorrow."

With that Fiona left her to wonder where the morning had gone, she checked her phone but there were no messages from Matt but maybe he was busy too, there was no way she was contacting him first. Treat them mean, keep them keen was the way she wanted to play this one, she liked him far too much to mess it up by being too obvious.

She half-heartedly went through a pile of paperwork Charlie had left on her desk but none of it looked important, it would keep until tomorrow. She wanted to get back into Eva's notebooks. She was enjoying this slice of social history.

She picked up the next book on the pile dated 1963 it went on in much the same vein as the previous one but there was a lot more detail about the people that used the library and day to day gossip, it felt like Eva was beginning to enjoy keeping a journal and was telling her life like a story. There were some real characters that used the library, old Henry who came in every day with his sandwiches and ate them whilst reading books on local history. She had liked him so let him get away with it although when anyone else tried to bring their lunch into the library she gave them short shrift. She would have young courting couples who would read poetry to each other and the middle aged ladies looking for the latest Barbara Cartland books but trying to make it look like they wanted something more highbrow. She took a special interest in a few of her readers as she mentioned them many times. It seemed that most of the town visited the library at least once a month and Eva was kept busy, she took on a part-time assistant in 1964 to help with the workload.

The next book carried on through 1964, there was gossip galore in 1964 and a new mayor was elected because the previous mayor Mr Briggs junior had been caught with his hands in the till at the Town Hall. According to Eva he was an old bluffer and he should have gone years ago anyway, he'd never been a patch on his father.

Her phone pinged; she had received an email on her personal account. Matt wanted to take her out on Saturday night to the theatre. She said a silent thank you and replied that she'd love to. She didn't care what they were going to see she just enjoyed spending time with him.

She packed up her books, she wanted to get some fresh air, she'd been cooped up in the office all day and achieved very little and she could start fresh again tomorrow.

Chapter Forty Six

There was a buzz around the tunnel today as Maria cut his hair for him and Tom made sure his clothes were spotless, they had little understanding as to why today was so important, they had heard him talk about Mary in the past but they couldn't comprehend how important this was to him, still they were all willing to help, one of the golden rules of the community was no-one questioned anyone's actions as long as no one was getting hurt. Jack had washed and shaved and put his best clothes on and he was as nervous as hell. Mary after all these years, what would he say, what would she say. Four times already he'd tried to leave the tunnel only to turn around and question what he was doing. Was this madness? Maybe, but it was what Peter had asked him to do. Even after racking his brains he couldn't think where Peter would have gone and he'd already walked to the telephone box and tried his home number three times but there was no answer. All he could do was what Peter had asked of him, to go and see Mary, his precious Mary after all these years; she might laugh at him that was if she even remembered him. That thought made it even more difficult to attempt the walk into town, what if she didn't remember him, after all it had been fifty years. He thought he was going mad with too many thoughts pushing their way to the front of his brain all at the same time. Excitement, hopes, fears and doubts fighting for superior position, he felt exhausted and he hadn't even made a decision on whether he should go or not yet.

He thought he should walk and think because if he stayed any longer he may lose his nerve altogether and just not go and he had to go because Peter had asked him to and Peter rarely asked him for anything. He needed to find Peter too but first he needed to calm down and start thinking rationally again.

He started the walk into town, the fresh air helped him to focus better on the task ahead, he was forming a plan and he needed to see it through. The town in the distance seemed to sparkle in front of him it took on whole new dimension now he knew his Mary was still there, he began to feel like a teenager again.

Chapter Forty Seven

Peter was feeling quite pleased with himself, he had dropped the letter off to Jack and got out of town before Jack could catch up with him, he was sure that Jack would go and see Mary now he had the information and it wouldn't have hurt asking to treat it as a last wish. He knew he shouldn't have used emotional blackmail but sometimes it was the only way and time was short for Peter now all he wanted was to see his friend happy. He was comfortably sitting in his hotel room in Bournemouth having a drink and watching the sea. He hadn't planned on visiting the coast but he had to get away from Charmsbury, he couldn't risk Jack seeing him or he would have too much explaining to do. It had taken him a lot of work to find Mary from a distance and he didn't want to explain his interfering to Jack just yet.

He'd had a close call when he was in Charmsbury and Mary had come into the café when he was writing his letter to Jack, if she'd have realised who he was it could have made everything very different but he supposed he looked very different now to how Mary would have remembered him. He had to push Jack into doing this for himself; he'd watched Jack pining for her for fifty years.

He was going to spend a few days on the coast enjoying the fresh air before he went back to see what was happening in Charmsbury.

Chapter Forty Eight

She got home and as soon as she'd made dinner she would be ready to put her feet up and watch the TV for the evening, after her fabulous night out with Matt she felt like a pyjama and wine evening in front of some mindless movie, she'd even stocked up on popcorn and chocolate. It was going to be the perfect lazy evening.

She got her books out of her bag and put them on the kitchen table moving to one side the ones she had already read, it was really interesting reliving the sixties through Eva's eyes. She picked up her phone to ring her Nan and see if she knew any of this stuff, it needed to be talked about. She spent 30 minutes on the phone to Mary chatting about her date last night, Mary wanted all of the details and Alex was happy to share, it had been a wonderful evening and after the update on her love life she mentioned a few people from back in the sixties and discussed Eva and how she had perceived the world around her. It turned out that Mary had used the library too and remembered some of the characters Eva had written about, it seemed to churn up a lot of memories, it always felt good to laugh and chat with her Nan and there was a lot of gossip from her too but nothing about the things Alex was looking for.

When they'd finished talking Alex started making some spaghetti for dinner, it was easy and she couldn't be bothered with anything more complicated. Whilst she waited for it to cook she flicked through the next notebook still in 1964, it seemed like that was a busy year she thought. There was talk of boys with long hair, a trend set by the Beatles and it seems there was uproar about it especially in this small town. There was some redecorating done in the library by a local boy and his friend, it seemed that Eva was quite fond of Jack and Peter she mentioned them many times, Jack was having a rough time with his family and she thought he'd like an excuse to spend some time away from them. She didn't think much of his family.

She had to stop there, the spaghetti was in danger of turning into a pan of stodge, it would just have to do and she tipped it into a bowl, added butter and pepper and poured the sauce over it and went back to the books.

The work at the library had looked really good when it was finished the boys had even painted cartoon characters on the walls to brighten it up for the kids and moved the bookcases around, Eva had wondered why they'd done that but it looked good when they'd finished. The children that used the library afterwards loved it and it encouraged lots of new young readers into the library if only to see the cartoons.

Then there was a gap of several weeks in the journal, it had been so consistent but suddenly stopped and then started again at the end of the year, it seems that Jack was the boy who had gone missing. Alex had read about him in the archives when she was looking into the missing people in Charmsbury. It also appeared that Eva had no time for the parents, she wrote that they didn't appear at all worried over his disappearance and that they'd said that he'd come back when he was ready, she had been disgusted by their attitude. The bosses that oversaw the library had tried to get her to move to a bigger, busier library but Eva was having none of it and just wanted to stay where she was, there was an implication that she may have known something about one of the bosses and used the information to keep her job in Charmsbury. Alex was really warming to Eva. Meanwhile the regulars were still getting up to their usual antics in the library and life went on as usual.

She stopped reading, finished her dinner, poured herself a glass of wine and went to look through her DVDs for a copy of Dirty Dancing, in her opinion the ultimate chick flick. She felt like a lazy night watching Patrick Swayze taking baby out of the corner. She put her feet up and enjoyed the movie.

Chapter Forty Nine

Matt was sitting at his desk, drumming his fingers on the arm of his chair not knowing what to do next, he was feeling frustrated with work but for once happy with his personal life but he knew it would get confusing with Alex, a police officer and a journalist it was always going to be a problem. It had started already, his frustration was due to the body in the park investigation, no-one had come forward to claim the body which in itself was very strange as the woman hadn't looked like she'd been living on the streets nor was she a known homeless person in the area, the only clues he had to finding out anything about the case had come from Alex and everything she had said had checked out so far, the only link was missing people and a baby. He knew he couldn't discuss the case with her especially after the last time they'd tried to discuss it and him accusing her of trying to embody Hercule Poirot, that had not been one of his finest moments and he could not go to her cap in hand and see what else she may have found out or if she might offer some help. If she did come in and help and forgive the things he'd previously said then he'd be the laughing stock of the station with the other officers, getting information from a journalist, they'd hang him out to dry especially if they found out he was seeing her too. So the case was going nowhere and he didn't know which way to turn next. He even considered phoning Mary as she always seemed to know what Alex was up to but then she would betray his nosiness to Alex and another row would ensue, what a mess.

She'd agreed to go out with him on Saturday; he'd just have to see if he could broach the subject then and hopefully she might just be okay about talking about it. He could only hope.

Chapter Fifty

He stopped at a phone box and tried Peter's number again to no avail, he thought he might have to invest in a mobile phone if Peter didn't show up soon, telephone boxes were disappearing from everywhere, it used to take him fifteen minutes to walk to the nearest public telephone box and after that there seemed like there was one on every corner but now he had to search them out, yes it was probably time to give in and purchase a mobile phone, he might have to walk a short distance to get any reception but that would be okay if it meant he could speak to Peter or just help to find him.

Now he had to pander to Peter's wishes and he was feeling terrified of what might happen. He walked toward the address written in the letter, so far he was fine there was plenty of time and quite a way to walk yet although the memories came flooding back with every step. The first time he had met Mary, how beautiful she had looked but to Jack Mary always looked beautiful there was never a moment that he thought any different, even when she was dressed for gardening she had done it with style and looked perfect. With every landmark he recognised his heart quickened and a fresh memory would surface. He walked past a new coffee shop and decided to give it a try and he was well aware he was putting off the inevitable but after fifty years he thought another half an hour wouldn't matter and he really needed to pull himself together, the sign outside promised the best coffee money could buy. He stepped into the cool interior, the air conditioning keeping the temperature down and offering a fresh feel, it was fitted out in old fashioned dark wood panelling with rustic chunky furniture and a mass of greenery. He ordered himself a macchiato he'd never had one before and it seemed like a day to take chances. He smiled to himself and went and found himself a seat in the corner behind a large green fern, he was glad of the privacy. He sat quietly and reread Peters letter he was still moved by all the things Peter had gone through that he had kept to himself, in fact Jack felt a little hurt and a measure of guilt that Peter felt as though he couldn't confide in him and now Peter was offering him more help, when it really should have been the other way around. Jack put the letter away feeling far too emotional to be out in public even if he was hidden by a huge fern. He finished his drink and made his way back into the warm daylight. It wasn't far now and his nerves were kicking in, he turned the corner into Farm Road and his pace slowed, he knew that the road turned into a dead end in a little under half a mile, whilst there was a small estate at this end of the road the furthest property was an old farmhouse, that had given the road its name and amazingly still to this day belonged to Mary. He couldn't believe that after all this time she was still in the same house, why hadn't she moved away and started a new life, they had talked a lot about leaving town and going somewhere more exciting. Many years ago her parents had sold off some of the land to builders so the estate could be built he had read about it in the local newspapers, his family would have been green with envy had they stayed around to see it happen but after Jonathon they didn't stay in town long and he had no idea where they had gone.

It was all very tasteful, nice little semi-detached modern houses with front gardens and shiny family cars parked on the drives. Jack remembered it when it was farmland and the road he was walking along now was little more than a track with high hedges either side of the road. He had walked this road many times when he was a young man, a young man in love; that was when the fear of what he was about to do really set in. His breathing became erratic and his heart was pounding, he stopped for a moment by a low wall and steadied himself he was just turning the final corner and he had taken the first glimpse of the farmhouse, there it was standing alone at the end of the road and he didn't feel like he could go any further. He took another few steps and saw the house full on, it had hardly changed and as he was preparing himself for the last few minutes' walk and trying to prepare what he might say when he got there, then he saw someone at the door, a young blonde haired woman, she appeared to be knocking on the door, the door opened and she walked in, he didn't see who opened the door but he knew it must have been his Mary. He turned and walked back the way he had come, he couldn't go there it was difficult enough to see Mary but if she had visitors then he really couldn't do it, it would have to be another day. Jack knew in his heart of hearts that he had just given up too easily but he would be back he promised himself and he had to promise Peter too. Tomorrow he'd try again.

Chapter Fifty One

She got into work on time again hoping to impress Charlie and get him back on side, she hated being in his bad books, he had left a short note about a local story that he wanted her to look into and make a start on for the weekend edition which was fine she glanced at what it involved, no problem she could write about shop openings and the economy in her sleep. So if she still had two days to do it she could have a read of the notebooks before starting it. She pulled the books out of her bag and turned to the next one on the pile.

This book appeared to suggest the start of the strange happenings in the library. There were still notes about the locals and some unusual requests for books and plenty of frivolous information, but then the first mention of something that had worried Eva, she had taken her lunch to work with her as usual and treated herself to a bottle of Cola, she didn't have it often as it was too fattening but it was a weakness of hers she explained, that day had been a busy one in the library and she hadn't had chance to eat all of her lunch and had left it in the staff room. The following morning she had arrived at work and noticed the chair out of place but thought nothing of that but when she went into the staff area her food from the previous day had gone and all that was left was an empty bag, an empty cola bottle and a banana skin. There had been no-one else there except for her and she was more than a little spooked. Nothing else was out of place. The next few days entries sounded cautious but nothing else seemed to have happened so she returned to writing about the day to day things in the library. As the book went on there were a few things that happened that were a little odd but she could explain them away to herself even though she knew she was making excuses she said that on occasions that toilets looked like they'd been used when she knew they were spotless the evening before and one morning she had got in and the staff room had been very warm as if the fire had been left on but she knew it hadn't, she inspected it and it was switched off and cold. She had left a flask of coffee one evening and it had been drunk by the following morning, she took to leaving jumpers and blankets in the staff room but they were never taken although they did smell different although she thought that could have been her imagination. That was all around the time the council had supplied some electrical equipment for the staff, the kettle and fridge was a nice surprise for Eva who was used to the basics of a chair, table and a fire.

There had been a local election around that time so Eva believed there had been money made available to the libraries in the county to upgrade and win local people over, there were now more up to date books available and lots of new ideas for renewing the buildings. She had hoped they wouldn't be messing around with her library too much, she liked it just the way it was and she didn't want her friendly ghost chased off she was becoming accustomed to unusual things happening and no longer felt uncomfortable about it. As she was putting some flyers on the news board she noticed that the poster showing a picture of the missing Jack and a plea for any information had gone and she hadn't remembered taking it down. She wrote that she had felt sad for Jack and hoped wherever he was he was happy, he deserved it after having to live with that family of his, she thought it hard to believe that he could have been their son, his brother Jonathon was another story altogether he was a chip off the old block and a thoroughly unpleasant boy. Eva thought that they hadn't seemed to worry too much about their boy and never showed any emotion over him, whenever she saw them it was as if nothing had changed if fact you'd never have believed that their youngest boy had run away from home and still not been found. Eva knew if it was her she would be frantic with worry.

Alex felt someone looking over her shoulder "Charlie, don't creep up on me, you startled me."

"How's that story coming along?"

"Ahhh … well… I've not exactly started it yet." She blushed.

"What are you doing then Alex, it seems you don't want to do much work at the moment. After one decent story do you think this place is too small for your talents now?" He didn't look happy.

"No Charlie it's not like that, it's just, well it's just that that story about the body has led on to so many other stories and I still think there's a link. Charlie I think there's a really big local story here."

"So what have you got so far? There must be plenty to tell because it seems to have been taking up all of your time or maybe it's just that policeman that's taking up your time. Just do the work I give you Alex or I'll have to get someone else in and send you back to the Charmsbury office, where they'll put you on tea duty." He rubbed his forehead as if she was his biggest headache.

"Charlie please just give me a little more time, I know there's more to this story and I promise I won't let you down on the stories you give me to do but please don't ask me to stop looking into this." She hated begging and could no longer look Charlie in the eye, he sounded so disappointed in her but she'd show him if he just gave her the chance.

"Ok, Ok Alex carry on with your story but don't forget about the other stuff too, I still want the stories I set for you and they must take priority. Deal?"

"Deal Charlie. Thank you." She sighed with relief as she watched him walk towards his office.

Chapter Fifty Two

Mary was spending the afternoon at home catching up with her housework, she often wondered how there could be so much to do when there was only her to make a mess but there always seemed like there was an endless list of things that needed doing around the house. In an ideal world she'd have a housekeeper and she could just sit in the garden and read and paint and do all the things she promised herself she would do when she retired but until she won millions on the lottery she'd just have to do the housework herself. She turned the radio up and got on with the cleaning.

Just as she had got on the step ladders to clean out the kitchen cupboards the last chore of the day there was a knock at the door, grateful for the interruption she answered it to find Alex on the doorstep looking quite miserable.

"Come in hunny, whatever's the matter?"

Alex poured out the story of her day and the altercation with Charlie, Mary soothed her by telling her not to worry and opened the tin that held the chocolate brownies, they never failed to put a smile on Alex's face.

"I saw your Mum today and she said she'd hardly seen you since you started on this story, maybe you need to pop in and say hi but before you do you'd better update me on how your story's going, if it's causing trouble at work you must think it's worth it."

Alex was only too pleased to tell her Nan all about the notebooks and Eva's thoughts on the weird goings on.

Mary sat and listened to what Alex was saying but the more she heard the quieter she got, it was as if her Granddaughter was bringing back all of her treasured memories with just the mention of Jack's name and she wasn't ready to share them with anybody. She could hardly believe that Alex was sitting there telling her about a young man called Jack who'd gone missing. She didn't know if she should tell her what she knew about the story or that she had known Jack so well but Alex had loved her Granddad and it felt wrong to be telling her that her own Nan had always been so very much in love with another man.

Mary was intrigued by the goings on in the library though but she couldn't help Alex much with that, Eva had suffered from dementia so maybe it had started earlier than anyone had thought and this was how it had manifested for her in her day to day circumstances, Eva had not been given to flights of fancy she was very matter of fact under normal circumstances. She looked over at the notebooks and picked one out of the pile and opened it, she sat there for a moment just looking at the inside cover.

"Alex... that design you were telling me about, did it look anything like this?" With that said she turned the book around to face Alex.

"That's exactly it!" She said excitedly "Nan, do you think she did know something? I knew there was more to this, and it's too much of a coincidence to be just a doodle."

Chapter Fifty Three

He ambled back home constantly berating himself, he felt like a stupid old fool for bottling out but the more he thought about things the more he didn't know how to explain things to Mary in fact there were some things he still couldn't explain to himself. He would need to think things through before he went back or maybe he was just making excuses to himself. If he wasn't so tired he'd go right back and sort this all out now, no that was definitely bravado speaking and yet another excuse. What he really felt like doing was going straight back to her and telling her everything but he wasn't going to do that either he was too tired; he hated getting old and tired, he missed the energy of youth. Tomorrow, he promised himself, tomorrow.

He had no appetite so didn't hang around with the others but when he got to his room he found Mark waiting for him sitting in his chair reading a book. Jack was surprised, in all these years no-one had come into his room without being invited and now to see the stocky, sandy haired young man gave him a bit of a shock. "Hello Mark what are you doing here?"

"Sorry to impose Jack but I wanted to talk to you away from the others." He looked at the book, closed it and put it back in its rightful place.

"What's up?" Jack was curious, he hung his jacket up as he spoke.

"I have to leave Jack."

"No one's keeping you here Mark, it's not a prison, we'll miss you, you've been a big help here, how long is it now?"

"13 years." He bowed his head.

"Are you sure you want to go? Aren't you happy here? Has something happened?" He looked at Mark and could see the boy as he was when he arrived here a shy, unassuming boy with little confidence; he'd said his Dad had beaten that out of him since he'd been six years old and he'd turned up at the community with Peter at the age of 17. He'd helped out with planting and cooking and always been there willing to help with anything that needed doing. Now he was thirty years old but sitting in the chair in the dim room he looked a lot like that boy again.

"I've never been happier anywhere Jack but I've done something stupid and I need to leave, I'll never forgive myself." He stared at his hands in his lap.

"Let me be the judge of that, you don't have to leave if you don't want to. What could you have possibly done that's so bad?"

He took a gulp of air "well when we took Ruby out to the park, you waited around for a while afterwards, well so did I. I didn't feel like coming straight back so I hung around in the park for a while then went to a café. It was a really cool café and it had computers, I came back here after a while but the next day I returned there and sat playing around on the computers, I was having fun Jack, I didn't realise how good they were now. So I set up an email and a twitter account and checked out the news on Ruby, it was so easy Jack, there wasn't much being said about it and that made me angry, she deserved to have a lot of respect so I sent a message on twitter, implying that this had happened before."

"Okay so that's not a crime, you were feeling emotional."

"No, you see the woman reporter, well I didn't know who she was straight away but she sent a reply, I didn't answer it Jack, I didn't want to be traced but I'd set up an email address and a couple of days later I emailed her to the address she'd put on twitter telling her the years that the bodies had been put out. It was me Jack that led her to write that story about us, I realised what I'd done after I read the story, I put us all in jeopardy and then I still sent another message taunting her. I'm so sorry Jack. If this place gets found I'll never forgive myself." He still didn't take his eyes away from his folded hands.

Jack didn't know what to say, he sat on the side of his bed and looked at Mark, hadn't he himself had times when he'd done daft things when he got bored or lonely, how could he be angry at Mark for being human and stupid. He looked up at Mark "You don't have to leave, we'll sort things out. It's up to you Mark but I'd like you to stay." Mark looked up at Jack with surprise "So you're not mad?"

"What would that achieve, you're one of the family here and I think you already feel bad enough without me adding to it. Now let me get some sleep but if you decide to go make sure you come and see me first Ok."

Mark got out of the chair, smiled at Jack and left the room. Jack lay down on his bed after an emotional day and quickly drifted off to sleep with thoughts of Mary running through his dreams.

Chapter Fifty Four

She went back to the office and tried to focus on the story she'd been given to write up, her mind kept wandering back to the notebooks but as much as she wanted to read the entries in them she knew Charlie wouldn't hesitate sending her back to small town Charmsbury and she couldn't go backwards. She finally finished the story and passed it on to Charlie, hoping it would be good enough for him, before she went home she wanted to use the archives to check up on Jack who was mentioned in the notebooks, she needed to know about him and his family from a source separate to Eva.

She settled herself in front of the archive computer and typed in 1965 missing persons Jack, which was all the information she had. In a split second the results came through. Jack Adams, aged nineteen years disappeared from his home in Charmsbury on the twenty third of July. She scrolled through to the newspaper article apparently he had just disappeared into thin air, there had been a few personal items missing but no clues, he didn't have many friends but those he did have had no idea where he had gone. A boy called Peter was interviewed on more than one occasion apparently Jack's closest friend and Alex remembered his name had been mentioned by Eva when the library was redecorated. She went through the articles day by day but there were no sightings, no rumours, the police had no idea where to look. The family as Eva had written didn't seem to be too worried all they had said was that he had been having a difficult time after a relationship that had ended and he'd come back when he'd licked his wounds. They actually said that to the journalist, Alex was astounded and beginning to understand why Eva hadn't thought much of the family.

She swapped computers and looked online for Jack now she had his last name. There were a couple of links to newspaper archives which she checked but they were essentially the same story, no story followed of him being found or him returning home. She clicked onto the second page of results and found a J Adams article dated 1981, this turned out to be a Jonathon Adams who was found dead thirty miles north of Charmsbury, it was reported that he had been murdered and he was the brother of Jack Adams who had gone missing in 1965. Alex remembered reading that Eva hadn't thought much of this boy. The family had given a televised plea for information and looked devastated but after watching the old footage they had made no mention of Jack, Alex could only think that maybe he had returned home and it had never been reported.

She needed to go back to the notebooks and see what information was left to find. She headed home for an evening of reading and pampering she had a big date tomorrow.

Chapter Fifty Five

She couldn't wait to get home and read more of the books but she had promised her Nan she would go and visit her Mum, she hadn't seen her since this story took over her life. It was too far to walk so she took her car and it meant she could get home sooner and get back to the books. It was good to see her family, they spent an hour catching up and her Mum was so pleased to hear that Patty was still the local midwife; memories of Alex as a baby were relived. There was a lot of interest in her work and her Mum made her go through every bit of the story and how she had pulled it all together, the family were treating her like a star. Her Mum told her that Nan had known the boy who went missing quite well but she didn't know any more about it than that, she supposed back then everyone in town knew everyone else one way or another but she did remember Nan saying that the family were not very nice people, although they hadn't deserved the trouble they got. Alex was touched that they were so proud of her and made a mental note to press her Nan for a bit more information. Her Mum was very happy to hear that Alex's love life was looking promising, she pressed Alex for more information on Matt which Alex was more than happy to oblige her with. She felt bad leaving so early but she had so much she wanted to do.

She stopped at her favourite Indian restaurant the Taj and picked up some food, she could never resist their chicken balti and it would save her from needing to cook, then she raced home to the books.

She sat at the kitchen table eating the curry from the containers, somehow they tasted better that way and she had a glass of wine by the side of her so far untouched. She picked up a book and started reading, this one was dated 1969/70 and as with all of the others she had made some notes about the locals and about her work Alex was no longer interested in these entries so skipped through them and she didn't have to look far to find the reference she was looking for. Eva had written about her ghost and the night she saw him.

'I'd been working late and just as I was locking up I was sure I saw a movement in the children's area, I passed it off as a trick of the light but just to be sure I finished locking up and went to the side window to look inside and what I saw stunned me, my ghost was Jack I saw him clearly as he walked through the lighter area of the lobby, taller and leaner but there's no doubt, I was torn between running back in or leaving him in peace. I opted for leaving him, he looked well enough. I just can't work out how he was getting into the library, tomorrow I'll try to find out.'

There was more in the same vein but she was obviously as intrigued as was Alex now. Alex needed to find out more about Jack and his family and she knew where to start with that line of questioning, she would go and see her Nan tomorrow.

According to the book Eva had gone into work the next morning and checked the children's area where Jack had appeared from and discovered a small door, some sort of cupboard door but with no handle, it had been hidden behind a bookcase, she couldn't believe she had never found this before.

She couldn't find a way to open it and reasoned that this was the only place he could have come in from. According to the entries she had tried many times to open the door but to no avail, eventually she gave up trying and was just relieved that Jack was still around and well. It appeared that she left plenty of food and drink in the staff room so that if he visited there would at least be something for him. She could ensure that he had a safe place to come if he needed it. It didn't seem like she even considered telling his parents, she was more interested in Jacks welfare not theirs. There was one entry that mentioned in a particularly cold winter she left him a big heavy coat with a note on it and when she got in the next day it had gone, in its place there was a drawing. She had no idea what it meant but she treasured it.

On one occasion she had seen his father and asked if he had heard anything from Jack and his reply had been 'Oh he's gone, he'll be back when he needs something' with that he walked off. Eva stopped feeling guilty about her knowledge and took it on herself to keep Jack's secret. She took it to her grave with her.

Alex had found her link but she still didn't know what it all meant she was just pleased that she was on the right track now.

Chapter Fifty Six

As the new day dawned Jack was coming to the realisation that his way of life couldn't carry on much longer, it seemed that everything was conspiring against his lifestyle, his friend needed him, Mark had given that journalist a lead and he had the information to see Mary again. He always believed things happened in threes and now his life was destined to change. He crossed the fields to the telephone box and tried Peter again but again there was no reply. There was nothing he could do about the reporter at that moment and he had no way of knowing what she might know about the community. The one thing he could do was to go and see Mary and this morning he felt more in control of his emotions so now was as good a time as any, he strode purposefully towards town. His determination lasted until he got as far as the coffee shop then the doubts started to seep in again, he kept telling himself to keep moving forward just keep putting one foot in front of the other, today he didn't stop for coffee he kept walking, he turned into Farm Road for the second time in two days and forced himself to keep walking, he came to the bend in the road and saw the house at the end, Mary's house and whilst looking confident he felt anything but, a little voice in his head kept telling him to turn back but a louder voice that sounded a little like Peter's told him to be a man and just maybe he'd find some happiness. He followed the voice that sounded like Peter's.

The house loomed larger with every step, from the outside it was a perfectly normal farmhouse, well-kept with a front garden full of beautiful flowers and a gravel path leading from the gate to the green front door. He stopped at the garden wall with his hand on the wooden gate and took a deep breath, and watched the beautiful flowers that were moving with the breeze creating a sea of colour. He opened the gate and made his way up the gravel path, he approached the door, there was no bell just an old fashioned wrought iron door knocker in the shape of fleur de lys and he reached up and knocked it hard three times against the door. Everything happens in threes he thought and waited. Time slowed, he waited for what felt like an eternity and heard nothing, he turned and looked at the garden again admiring its beauty then from behind him he heard the door open and he was afraid, he had to force himself to turn around and face whoever had opened the door.

"Hello can I help you?" It was Mary's voice and as she spoke he turned around to face her. They stood looking at each other for a few seconds which felt like an eternity, he needn't have worried, she knew who he was. "Jack" It was almost a whisper "Jack, is it really you?"

Relief swept over him and he smiled at her, his Mary still as beautiful as ever. For a moment neither of them knew what to say to each other they just looked and took in what was in front of them. Mary looked wonderful to Jack, her hair was no longer blonde but now a beautiful silver with a white streak at the front, she still had a wonderful figure and looked every bit as beautiful to him in maturity as she had as a girl, he knew he hadn't fared so well but there she was smiling right back at him.

"Come in, we have so much to talk about, why are you here? Where have you been?" The words tumbled from her mouth as if she needed to say everything at once.

Jack still at a loss for words just gently leaned forward and kissed her cheek something he'd dreamed of doing for fifty years. It silenced her and she led the way into her house, smiling. Jack closed the door behind them.

Chapter Fifty Seven

She had been eager to get some shopping done that morning but got side-tracked by trying to find out more about Jack Adams. There didn't seem to be anything on the internet that she didn't already know, the only other references to the family were the stories about Jonathon but that could wait. She had a big date tonight and she wanted to pick up a killer outfit to make up for not making enough of an effort last time. She needed to talk to her Nan too and find out if her Mum was right and she had known Jack, maybe she could offer some information that Alex didn't already know although she couldn't imagine why her Nan hadn't mentioned that she had known Jack. She would ring her later and see what she knew.

She went out into town and headed towards the nice end of town with the best shops, to get to them she had to go past the library and it occurred to her that just maybe she could go in and have a snoop around whilst touching base with Sandra. She went in and looked around but couldn't see Sandra so she made her way towards the children's section. There was a small group of six or seven year olds sitting in a circle on the floor listening to a young woman reading to them, she was pretty good at the voices too, Alex remembered when she was a kid sitting in the same place listening to stories, it was nice to know some things didn't change. She made her way over to the bookcases and started looking for the door that Eva had written about but all she could see was bookcases. She looked around for Sandra again and spotted her sitting with a man looking through index cards, she waited until she was free.

"Hello Sandra, I just popped by to say thanks for your help, Tony was a great help too and those notebook are invaluable, please tell him I'll get them back to him soon."

"Don't rush love, they'd only be taking up space in our house, we've not bothered reading much of them."

"Really…. they're really interesting, you should."

"Can I help you with anything today?"

"Actually I hope you can, there's a reference in one of the books to a cupboard door and I'd like to take a look at it if I could."

"Oh you mean the door that isn't, well that's what we call it because it just doesn't open, I'd almost forgotten about that, yes it's over here, come and have a look, It'd be good if you could tell us what it was for because we've never worked it out." She strode across the library to the bookcase that Alex had already looked at and gave it a hearty push, gradually the bookcase started to move across enough to reveal the door. Just as Eva had said it was small and looked like it was for a small cubby hole, just a place to store a few old boxes or something, the only problem was it had no handle or obvious way of opening it. "That's it there, any idea how to open it?"

"No sorry, the books didn't give up that secret, but I'm glad I've seen it for myself. You could make a feature of that with all the popular fantasy books that are around for kids at the moment." It was quite a cute little door and Alex could just imagine a group of hobbits knocking at it awaiting an adventure.

"You're not the first to say that, maybe we could have done but the council are moving the library soon to a newer building so there's no point now."

"What will happen to this building?"

"No idea, it seems no-one's interested in it as far as I know, but the council never tell us anything. It's a lovely place, I'll miss it here but the new building will be warmer and more modern. Probably cheaper for the council in the long run." Sandra gestured towards some people who had just entered the library.

"Thanks for your time, tell Tony I'll see him soon."

With that Alex left the library to go shopping down by the sea front and check out the shops where she could seriously treat herself, she was looking forward to this evening.

Chapter Fifty Eight

They sat in the kitchen in a pool of sunlight which was coming through the open window, Mary had opened a bottle of wine and they sat opposite each other both nervously playing with their glasses. They looked at each other for minutes without saying a word it was almost as if a spell would be broken if they spoke, in truth neither of them knew what to say but they were enjoying the pleasure of being able to just be near each other after all this time.

Mary reached over and took Jack's hand, looked into his still baby blue eyes, just as she remembered them and broke the silence "I'm sorry."

"No Mary, how else could it have ended and we both knew it had to end."

"Where have you been? Do you have a family? Have you been happy?"

"I was not as lucky as you Mary but I suppose the people I surrounded myself with could be called my family. Are you happy? "

Mary told Jack about her life with Geoffrey and what a good husband and father he had been and about her children, Janet who lived in town with her own grown up family and Christopher who had emigrated to New Zealand some years ago with his new wife and about the loneliness of losing her husband. How her life had gone and that yes she had been happy but had always missed Jack, there hadn't been a single day she hadn't thought of him.

Jack was just about to start telling her about his life when the phone rang, it made him visibly jump it wasn't a sound he was used to, Mary let go of his hand and went to answer it, he overheard the one side of the conversation and got the feeling he was being talked about but no-one else knew he was here so he must be wrong. Mary came back and took her seat again and took his hand immediately as if he might disappear if she wasn't holding on to him, she didn't want to lose him again. "Sorry about that, my granddaughter just asking a few questions about the past."

"I heard my name, did you tell her I was here or who I was?"

"No but it was about you, her Mum had mentioned I knew you and she wanted to know a little about you."

"Why would she know or even want to know about me? How does she even know I exist?" Jack felt confused.

"She's writing a story and your name turned up as a missing person along with a few others, quite a coincidence don't you think?"

Jack mentally put two and two together. "Your granddaughter wouldn't be called Alexandra by any chance?"

"Yes do you know her?" Mary couldn't believe he knew someone else in her family.

"No, only her name, Alexandra Price, local journalist. Mary I don't think I should be here, maybe this was a mistake," He suddenly felt very sad.

"No Jack I let you go once, I won't do it again. What's wrong? What have you done?" She felt all the old feelings stirring again and she was determined that she wouldn't let him just walk out of her life.

Jack took a deep breath and started to explain what happened in his life after they had split up, how he hadn't coped well and had decided to run away and had been living in a tunnel not three miles from here for the past fifty years. Mary listened in silence finding it hard to believe that he'd been so close for all of these years whilst her life went on as normal, in fact she was finding the whole story hard to believe, how he could have lived like that for most of his life she needed to understand. He told her about Peter and how he had helped and still was helping and had it not been for him they wouldn't be sitting there together now. Mary suddenly remembered the man in the café writing a letter that had looked so familiar it had been Peter.

They sat in the kitchen with their untouched wine talking for hours and it was starting to get dark outside. Jack still hadn't told her about his connection to Ruby but he knew he would have to at some stage and Mary knew he was holding parts of his life back from her but they both knew they had all the time in the world to catch up on all of the details.

They relaxed enough to enjoy the wine eventually and raised their glasses as a toast to themselves and recaptured love.

Jack reluctantly got up to leave; Mary made him promise that he would be back that he wouldn't just walk out of her life now. It was a promise Jack was happy to make.

Chapter Fifty Nine

She had rung her Nan before she had started to get ready for her night out and got the impression she was intruding on her Nan's afternoon, it felt as if she hadn't wanted to talk to her for long and was making excuses to get off the phone, especially after she had directly asked about Jack, Peter and Jonathon. Did her Nan know something about Jack Adams or the others that she didn't want to rake up all these years later? That was how it had felt. Alex didn't have too much time to worry about it she needed to get ready for her second date with Matt and again she had butterflies and she knew exactly why, she was falling for him, the tall, handsome police officer had stolen her heart and she didn't want to fight it any longer.

He picked her up looking as handsome as ever even though he'd abandoned the suit this time he was wearing black jeans and an open neck shirt and he looked good enough to eat, they went straight out, they only had just over an hour to get to the theatre and were hoping to fit in a drink before the show started. They made it in plenty of time for a relaxing drink, Alex initially thought Matt had his mind elsewhere but he soon settled into the evening, she was pleased to see other women looking him up and down with approving glances and obvious disappointment when he took her hand to lead the way to their seats. The show was hilarious, initially she had thought 'The Importance of Being Earnest' was going to be a stuffy old fashioned play but they had laughed so much it had turned out to be a wonderful evening. After the show they walked through the town looking for somewhere to eat and found a quiet little Chinese restaurant that served the best sake she had tasted in a long time. They talked about their lives and their families and the things they loved to do outside work. Then suddenly Matt's mood changed leaving Alex wondering what she had done wrong. He seemed to be trying to change the conversation around to their jobs but obviously not knowing how to approach the subject. The food provided a distraction for a short while until Alex couldn't put up with it any longer.

"Matt if you have something to say, just say it."

"Well…" he faltered "Well, I was just wondering how the story was going, have you come up with a theory yet?" He looked at her sheepishly.

"I have some ideas, is this what bringing me out again was all about? Do you want to know what I've discovered? Haven't you got your own ideas?" She was starting to feel her blood pressure rising, she had genuinely thought he liked her, how could she have got it so wrong. They had agreed not to discuss work and now it seemed that he had nothing on the case so he was trying to find out what she knew. He had a nerve after telling her she was interfering in police work and playing amateur detective trying to make him look stupid.

"No, really I am just interested in your take on it or if you've found out who dunnit?" He covered his embarrassment well by trying to make a joke of it.

"Interested in my work or interested in any information you could get out of me? You should know more than me you are the one with the man power and the intelligence as you made very clear to me." Alex could feel herself getting angry this was not how she had expected the evening would play out. "Couldn't you have asked me for information by ringing me up? Did you have to wait until we were having a perfectly nice evening?" Without giving him a chance to reply she got up, put her coat on and left the restaurant, she knew he was trying to follow her but he had to settle the bill first and it just gave her enough time to flag down a passing taxi and leave him standing only able to look at the back of her taxi disappearing down towards Charmsbury.

Chapter Sixty

Mary woke up smiling, she hadn't felt this good for a long time, she wanted to tell the world that Jack was back but knew for a little while longer she would have to keep that information to herself, she needed to know the part of the story that Jack had not told her. She was looking forward to getting to know him all over again. She went about her day with an unusual feeling of completeness and hoped she would see Jack again very soon. As she stepped out of the shower she heard the phone ring she wrapped her dressing gown around her and went downstairs.

"Hello Nan" She sounded miserable, what had happened?

"Hi hunny, what's wrong? You sound like you're upset."

Alex told her about how wonderful the previous evening had been and how things had deteriorated so quickly by the end.

"Just wait until you hear from him, he'll be in touch I'm sure, he probably feels every bit as bad this morning as you do, you'll work it out." She tried to calm Alex down but it didn't seem to have much effect on her.

"Nan he used me just to find out about the story... and I really liked him."

"I can't believe that Alex, he really likes you too maybe he was just clumsy the way he approached the subject, maybe he was expecting you to react like you did which was why he had to think it through for so long."

"So you're on his side then" That was when the tears really started, Mary didn't know what to do.

"I'm not on anyone's side, I just don't think you should think the worst of him for asking a question, ring him Alex see what he has to say."

"No he can ring me." Alex was too stubborn for her own good. "Can I come and see you this afternoon Nan?"

"I'm going out later, sorry I won't be here, maybe tomorrow? Ok?"

"Ok" that was all Alex could say she was a bit shocked, her Nan had never refused her anything before.

Mary got off the phone feeling lousy about not inviting Alex round but aware that if Jack came back today he would not be ready to meet the family and she felt a little guilty that she wanted him all to herself for a while, at least until they had caught up properly and she thought there was a lot of things that Jack hadn't told her yet.

Chapter Sixty One

He woke up feeling amazing, he'd forgotten how good it felt to be in love and he was just learning that these feelings are not just for teenagers but they did make you feel like one. He smiled to himself as he got out of bed and did some exercises, he wanted to get ready and get back to Mary as soon as he could, they'd been apart for too long and there was so much to catch up on, yesterday hadn't done more than scratch the surface. There was something that worried him and that was Alexandra, he hadn't told Mary the darker side of his life and it appeared that Alexandra was learning more about him all the time with Mark's help. He had no idea how this would resolve itself but he wanted to see Mary again and he had made her a promise that he wouldn't disappear again. He went out to the well to sit and think things over for a while, it was too early to turn up at Mary's yet and he needed to work out how he was going to tell his story. It was a mess but he was determined not to lose Mary again over it. He was sitting with his back against the well, he tilted his head backwards to the sun and deeply breathed in the morning air and felt himself relax, it felt good to be alive today.

He'd washed and showered and was making his way towards town, he'd sent Mark out to buy a mobile phone for everyone to share but mainly because he wanted to keep trying to get hold of Peter without having to walk to the phone box every hour. Mark seemed the right choice to send having proved his up to date knowledge of technology and he had been eager to try to do something to make amends to Jack.

Jack approached Mary's house but today he felt no trepidation, only happiness and love. She was waiting for him, she had cooked for him and they sat down to a wonderful late lunch and more wine and again they talked. She showed him around her garden and was pleased that he knew all about the plants and herbs she was growing, she had held on to quite a large plot of land behind the farmhouse and she was proud of her garden. They walked back into the house and eventually they got around to talking about the things that he had missed out telling her the previous day, he knew he just had to tell her the truth or they would never be able to move forward.

"I'm not proud of everything I've done Mary but there was a reason for all of it." She handed him a piece of cake "Before I try and explain it all to you would you come and see where I live?" He thought she may understand more if she could feel a part of it. "This cake is amazing."

"I'd like to see your home Jack, it's hard to imagine it from what you've told me so far and stop trying to change the subject." She looked directly at him. "What happened to your family?"

"Honestly I have no idea, I heard they moved away but I don't know where and I care even less."

"Really? And what about your brother?"

He didn't know how to answer "He's dead Mary, that's when the family moved away, they couldn't cope losing their favourite son, that's all I know" He felt like a coward for not coming clean but how could he tell her.

"Did you ever see them again?"

"I saw glimpses of them around the town but I never spoke to them after the day I left, why would I, they never cared if I had lived or died. You know what they were like Mary, you felt their wrath more than once."

Mary left the questioning there, it wasn't going to help either of them move forward talking about ancient history and there was certainly no love lost between her and his parents.

With that small awkwardness out of the way they continued discussing the people they had known and catching up on what each other had been up to in their day to day lives. They had been talking for so long Jack was shocked to notice that it was already getting dark.

"Meet me at the phone box on Hill Street tomorrow noon Mary, I want to show you my home, I'm hoping you'll like it there"

"I'd love to." She smiled "You don't need to go back tonight, you can stay here."

"Not tonight, know more about my life before we take things any further" He felt a little foolish but said what he was thinking anyway "I love you Mary and another day or two after fifty years of longing can only make life sweeter."

"I love you too, I always have."

Chapter Sixty Two

Alex didn't know what to do with herself today, she got the bus to work half-heartedly, and she couldn't believe that only forty eight hours ago she had been looking forward to a night out, her love life had been on the up and she had been filled with excitement about her story. Now she felt flat, no love life, nothing new on the story and she was suffering from a severe lack of interest in everything, she hadn't even heard from Matt. It felt like this was going to be a long day and she knew she'd have to put some work in on whatever Charlie had picked out for her to cover today. She was feeling sorry for herself and didn't even get the chance to talk things over with her Nan.

She got into work and sure enough there was a pile of paperwork for her to work through about a local politician and his expectations for the coming year, she really was having some doubts about this job. Just as she got the files out and started to read up on Mr Stephen Smyth, Layla's head popped round her partition and thrust a huge bunch of flowers at her.

"These just came for you."

"Wow thank you, where did they come from?"

"They were left at reception for you, Sarah didn't know if you were in or not so she took them in. They're from a proper florist too, not through the internet. You must have impressed somebody." She gave Alex a huge grin and went back to her own desk.

Alex put them on her desk and hunted through the foliage and white roses to look for a card, it was a handwritten note the size of a business card with just two words on it 'I'm sorry' She smiled, the day was looking better already, she hoped there would be an email soon too, if not she would ring Matt tonight and thank him and tell him he was forgiven.

Feeling better about the day she picked up her phone and arranged an appointment with Mr Stephen Smyth to discuss his hopes and fears for the local elections and turned back to Eva's books. There was only two books left to read and she tore through them looking for any more information, again there were lots of stories about the regular readers, people asking for obscure books and just the odd note about things being moved around also books she had lost turning up inexplicably. Then there was a note about the sticker in the window, she had been out for the day with her husband and seen a window sticker that was almost the same design as the drawing that had been left for her by her ghost, she bought it and stuck it on the library window just because it made her smile and she secretly hoped that Jack might see it. There didn't seem to be anything else substantial that would help her story. Alex piled them up on the desk ready to return them to Tony, it would be nice to see him again and she was pleased the mystery of the sticker had been resolved; she could return them without wondering if she'd missed anything. She decided she would have an early finish and take the bus out to her Nans and see if she could offer any more information, she needed to find out why her Nan hadn't mentioned knowing Jack Adams.

It wasn't quite lunchtime so if she hurried she could get to her Nan's well before lunch and get the best of whatever she had been cooking that morning, her stomach groaned with anticipation.

Chapter Sixty Three

Mary was ready and excited about what the day might bring, she felt like a kid going out on her first date. Jack had told her not to dress up but make sure she had some good walking shoes on, the anticipation of this coming afternoon was making her jittery. She got her comfortable shoes out and dressed in jeans and an oversized T-shirt, she added a little make up and she was ready to go. The walk to the telephone box where she would meet Jack was lovely, it was a cooler day today it seemed like the heat of recent weeks may be coming to an end. She stood at the phone box and waited. Within five minutes Jack crept up behind her and put his arms around her, she gave in to him immediately; it felt so good to be loved again. They strolled out towards the nature reserve hand in hand; she wasn't feeling shy and didn't care if anyone saw her she was just happy. She hadn't been out in this direction for many years, it was always the tourists that headed to the nature reserve, the locals rarely bothered with it.

"Where are we going Jack?" She asked as they veered away from the reserve and towards some scrubland.

"Shhh just trust me, come on" He felt like a kid, finally showing off his discovery to someone he cared about. They walked across the scrubland. "Can you see anything? Tell me what you're thinking."

"I see trees and hedges, there's nothing else here, no, wait, it looks like there's a shack over there." She pointed to their outhouse which really was no more than a shack and mostly hidden by bushes and trees but when you looked carefully you could just make out the roof, in the winter it was more obvious. He turned to the right veering away from the shack.

"It looks like people have been walking around here and look a well, is this the well you told me about?"

The very same, I spent a lot of time here thinking about you, come on lets go in, there's some people who can't wait to meet you."

"What...."

He walked around a bush full of blackberries and she plucked one from the bush as she passed, it was sharp and the flavour exploded in her mouth, she followed him to be confronted with a sloping hole, he helped her down the wooden steps that had been put in to make it safer to get in and out, she entered the tunnel and couldn't believe what she was seeing, stone and wood walls and ceiling, the floor was compacted dirt with stones set in it, it was like something out of a book. She was speechless she just followed Jack, it seemed to go on for long distance, there were pictures drawn and painted on the walls several of them were the same design as Alex had been trying to find out about, loops with a heart set in the centre and there were material hangings over what she assumed were doorways, she didn't know where to look first and then he turned into what she could only describe as a recreation area. There were several people milling around preparing food in a half light of stick on battery lamps, they were stuck on any surface that would hold them but they threw a warm low light, everyone in the room in turn looked up and welcomed her with warm honest smiles, she was made to feel like a very special guest.

Jack took her through the dining area and a little further along to a room that even seemed to surprise Jack when he got there.

He opened the door to his room and was astonished to see the room ablaze with candles, cushions had been thrown all over his bed to make it look more like a settee, everywhere was spotlessly clean and a bottle of wine had been placed on his bookcase next to the empty 'Chance" bottle. Mary watched his reaction to how beautiful this cave room had been made to look, she stepped towards the perfume bottle and picked it up and smiled at Jack "You really are soft, I can't believe you still have this. This room looks lovely, Oh Jack have you really lived here all of this time? It's so magical and beautiful."

"Always here but it's never looked this good." He smiled "It's never had you here before."

He explained how life had led him here and the reasons he stayed, Mary was stunned to learn of all the people who had been here yet nobody in town knew this place existed "You and Peter did all of this?"

"Well honestly, this place was nothing like this until the others moved here, it was them that made it a good place to be. They love Peter here and that's why we need to find him and bring him back, I still have no idea where he is?"

Chapter Sixty Four

Alex managed to catch the early bus, as she was getting close to her Nans she decided to call her to see if there was anything she needed picking up, the phone just rang out her Nan wasn't in. Alex wished she'd rung earlier now but it was so unusual Nan rarely went out without mentioning it when they chatted, which made her remember how her Nan had sounded on the phone the last time they spoke. She'd have to ring her later and find out what was going on. She locked her phone and dropped it in her bag and looked out of the window trying to decide what she was going to do with her afternoon now. She saw a familiar figure walking just off the road, it looked just like her Nan but it couldn't be. This woman was wearing jeans and a T-shirt her Nan would never have gone out dressed like that and there was a man with her, holding her hand. Alex couldn't believe what she was seeing no it couldn't be right, why would she be going to the nature reserve with a man. Alex was stunned, her Nan hadn't mentioned a man in her life but she had sounded weird on the phone yesterday. Alex grabbed her flowers and rang the bell for the bus to stop, great, she'd managed to find a driver that was a stickler for the rules and made her wait until they had reached the bus stop, she walked back up to where she had seen the man and woman but there was no sign of them, she walked over to the nature reserve where she was sure to find them, there was nothing else out this way. Alex walked around the nature reserve for over an hour but couldn't see them and they certainly couldn't have missed her carrying a large bouquet of white roses around reluctantly, she didn't want to dump the flowers but they were a nuisance, then she finally gave up and walked back towards town more than a little perplexed.

She eventually went home and tried to phone her Nan again but still no answer she was beginning to worry. She sent Matt a thank you email for the flowers and settled back to watch TV for a while but couldn't stop thinking about her Nan.

Two hours later the phone rang and invaded her particularly vivid dream she was having about fish and monkeys, she reached out for her phone and saw it was her Nan's name flashing on the screen.

"At last, where have you been?" She sleepily mumbled into the phone.

"Just been out for a walk, why? I noticed I missed a couple of calls is everything ok?'

"Yes fine, I was worried about you, did you go to the nature reserve today?"

"Yes I decided to go for a walk, it's beautiful out there you know."

"I know Nan, I tried to find you after I saw you from the bus but you disappeared. Who was your friend?" She knew she sounded sulky but she thought she was justified she had been worried.

"Oh just someone I met on the way, I just fancied a walk."

Alex could have sworn she could hear a smile in her Nan's voice but let it go they would only end up arguing and if she didn't want to tell there was nothing Alex could do. "Can I come over and see you tomorrow?"

"Of course you can I'll be in until 3pm, have you heard from that man of yours yet?"

Alex told her what had happened and how beautiful the flowers were and that she was still waiting to actually speak to him. They gossiped for a few minutes and agreed to see each other the next day. Alex put the phone down even more confused now but at least everything was okay and she no longer had a reason to worry and she would find out who the man was, she would just have to wait until tomorrow.

Chapter Sixty Five

Peter had had enough of looking at the endlessly blue sea, he had walked around the small town and seen what all of its shops were selling, had a drink in its seafront pub and eaten local fish and chips and thought it was time to go back home now. He had experienced all it had to offer and had seen enough, he no longer had enough time left to hang around places for no reason, he had a few arrangements still to make, paperwork to take care of and a hospital visit to go to in a couple of days, he was looking forward to going home and the comforts that only home could provide, he knew Jack would have been trying to ring him but he hoped that by now Jack might have other things to discuss with him aside from his illness when they spoke. He was hoping his interference was working out, if it was then his debt to Jack had been repaid. He smiled and whistled to himself as he packed his bag, he hadn't felt this good in a long time and he was going to enjoy the drive home, the sea air must really be doing him some good after all.

Chapter Sixty Six

He was happy, truly the happiest he had been for many years and now Mary had experienced a little bit of life in the community and it appeared that she liked it, in fact she seemed enthralled by it and that made him happy too, he hoped she would come back again and get to know the other people he shared his life with. Life was turning out to be good, finally. They were going to meet up today at 4pm in the park and go for a meal later but Jack was eager to see her again so thought he would surprise her at home and walk with her to the park, he might even take her some flowers. He was also aware that he would have to share the downside of this way of life too, she may not want to know him once she knew about the bodies and what he'd done to his brother, he didn't want to tell her but it wouldn't be fair to carry on without being honest with her and giving her the whole picture. The community wasn't quite as magical as she would wish to believe; in fact some of the things they had to deal with weren't very pleasant at all. He decided tonight he would lay his cards on the table and hope that she understood and could forgive the things he had to do to keep the community safe.

Jack went to find Mark who had been left in charge of setting the mobile phone up for them and then he could try Peter again. He found Mark out by the well playing with the phone.

"Have you managed to get it working yet?"

"Yes it's ready to go, I chose this one it's easy to use and not too fancy, is it ok?" He was still being careful around Jack and it showed. He handed Jack the small black phone.

"Is that it? It's tiny. Does it work?"

"Yes but you'll need to walk up towards the road to get a signal, there's nothing here. You won't need to go as far as the phone box though."

"Let's try it out" They walked around watching to see if the little bars on the phone would light up and Mark had been right, just before they got to the road the bars appeared and with every metre they walked the reception got stronger. Mark showed him how to use it and walked away so Jack could make his call. It rang out loud and clear but there was no answer from Peter, Jack would just keep trying he sat down in the grass and waited, daydreaming and watching a few clouds drift by to fill the time and he tried again, still nothing.

He made his way back; he needed to get ready to pick Mary up. He had sorted out the best of his clothes again and tonight he would treat her to the best he could afford.

With some trepidation he made his way to town, he stopped at a florist and picked up a bunch of red roses hand tied with ribbons and shiny paper, he's never bought flowers for anyone before and it was a good feeling. He made his way to the cottage, it was 3.15pm and as he got to the bottom of the road he saw the blonde woman leaving the house the same woman who he had seen visiting the first time he came, he wondered who she was and hung back until she was clear of the cottage, whoever she was he wasn't ready to meet her just yet.

She opened the door and found Jack behind the beautiful roses and she seemed very pleased to see both of them. He followed Mary into the house and waited whilst she put the flowers in water, cooing over how beautiful they were whilst inhaling the fragrance, she came back into the lounge with the roses beautifully displayed in a cranberry glass vase and placed them on the mantelpiece, he felt proud and couldn't love this woman more if he'd tried.

"Who was that just leaving?"

"Oh that was Alex, I thought I should get her out of the way early so I could get ready, just as well I did. I'm not sure you want to meet the family journalist yet." She smiled at him.

They sat talking and trying to decide where they should go for dinner, after much discussion of the merits of restaurants many of which he had never heard of let alone set foot in, Mary suggested they go shopping and then stay in, she would cook for him. It sounded perfect to him and they could talk more openly without the distraction of other diners. The shopping was fun and the meal was delicious, no restaurant could have topped the food he had that evening. They talked about all manner of things and laughed more than he could ever remember laughing in his life. He wanted to put off the discussion he knew he had to have with Mary but it seemed there would never be a right moment to bring the subject up.

"I know this may spoil a perfect evening but we really need to talk." He found it difficult to keep eye contact with her.

"What's wrong, I thought we were having a good time?"

"I keep putting off this conversation but there are things you need to know before we go any further, you may not want to stay around once you know." Sadness tinged his voice.

"I don't think there's anything......" She began to say but got cut off in mid-sentence.

"Mary, I've done things that have been unpleasant and inexcusable and I won't build a relationship on anything but the truth."

She poured them a glass of wine; they sat opposite each other across the dining table and he began to tell her about his family and the times when people had started to live with him at the tunnel. She never took her eyes off him all the while that he spoke, he was grateful that she just listened, he thought had she interrupted he may not be able to get through this account of his life. He told her about what he had to do when people died and that the body in the park was Ruby and he had put her there. Mary still sat and listened, finally he told her about the altercation with his brother that ended in his death, although he had to admit he had no idea how Jonathon's body ended up 30 miles away but he had never questioned it. He had killed his own brother by beating him with a rock; he still believed he had been justified in attacking him but not for killing him. At that Mary did show some emotion but still she said nothing. Finally exhausted he drained his wine and made to leave.

She put out her hand and gently touched his arm to stop him from leaving. "Don't go Jack, I need to take all of this in but I don't blame you for anything that's happened. You put those bodies out so at least their families could have a chance of saying their goodbyes, apart from your brother I can't see that you've done anything wrong and if you say you had good reason I believe you. You offered people an opportunity of a happy life and from what I saw the people who are there do seem happy. Does Peter know about your brother?"

"Peter was there when it happened, I think Jonathon had caught sight of Peter and followed him to me, he came into the tunnel, shouting that he was going to send the police in and he started pushing the women around and calling them filthy names and trying to touch them, I told him to leave and I thought he had and then I caught sight of him forcing himself on a young woman, he'd got her pushed up against the wall with one hand around her neck whilst he was raping her I couldn't let him do that and I couldn't let him call the police, he pulled a knife on me and it all escalated from there." Jack looked broken. "How could I do that to my own brother Mary, how?"

"Jack...." Mary didn't know what to say, she couldn't condone his actions but Jonathon was truly a nasty man, there were no words, she got up out of her chair and walked round the table and held Jack until he stopped crying.

Chapter Sixty Seven

Mary had a lot to think about, Jack had stayed with her overnight, they had slept on top of the bed just holding each other, it was wonderful to wake up and the first thing she saw was his messed up white hair, she just lay next to him and watched him whilst he slept, watching his chest steadily rise and fall and hearing his gentle even breathing, eventually she had to tear herself away, she needed a shower sleeping fully dressed had left her feeling very uncomfortable, she left Jack to sleep he looked so peaceful. When he woke up they had a small breakfast together and he went back to the community, he thought she should have time to think about what she was getting herself into.

She had spent some time cleaning but couldn't settle to a task so she went out into the garden; a little light gardening always helped her think. She processed all the information Jack had told her last night but still couldn't believe that Jack could kill someone. Alex was coming very close to finding out about Jack and she didn't want that to happen. She wouldn't be able to put Alex off as she just kept finding out more and more and was certainly getting closer by the day. The one thing that didn't take any time to work out was that there was no way that she was going to let Jack go now they had finally found each other again.

She was forming a plan but she needed to go and see Jack before she did anything else, they did this together or it wouldn't work.

She walked across the scrubland out towards the tunnel hoping Jack would be there when she got there also hoping she could find it again, she had to try. As luck would have it she saw one of the women she had met when she visited with Jack she thought her name was Sam, she was tall and pretty but had a long scar down one side of her face. Mary couldn't help but wonder what had happened to her in the past. She was dressed in jeans and an old lumberjack shirt; they greeted each other warmly and chatted for a minute about some of the people she had met on her last visit. She explained that she needed to see Jack and Sam walked with her to the tunnel, it was a relief to have someone with her who knew where they were going. Sam took her into the recreation area which today was busy with three adults trying to teach two children mathematics, they were having a lot of fun doing it if the giggling going on was anything to go by, Sam made her a drink then she went off to find him. She returned about fifteen minutes later followed by Jack looking like he'd just woken up. He looked at her, he showed no emotion, Mary smiled and he returned it tenfold and wrapped his arms around her.

"Now it's my turn to talk." She said as she allowed him to hold her in a tight embrace.

"Let's go outside and sit by the well, it'll be private out there." He looked around at the people in the room, they had all heard and one or two of them nodded at him, he held her hand as he led her outside.

They settled themselves on the grass with their backs to the well wall, Mary couldn't believe how young she felt being here, it felt so natural.

"Jack I've been thinking and there's a couple of things we must sort out, you know my granddaughter Alex is still working on the body in the … sorry… Ruby's story. I think you two should meet."

"I can't do that, she'd write the story then I'd be arrested for the bodies and for my brother, I can't go to prison." He looked defeated already.

"That could be a problem alright; her boyfriend is a police Inspector."

"That makes it even worse… I'm not warming to your idea so far." He managed a grin.

"Talk to Alex, let her have your story she won't print everything and she may not have to use your name but she could put your side of the story make it emotive, you killed your brother but only in self-defence they won't lock you up for that."

"No strictly true and she'd want to come here and that would open all of these good people up to having to go back on the streets and fend for themselves. You've seen for yourself how well this community works, I can't do that to them Mary, it wouldn't be fair."

"We wouldn't have to tell her about this place." Then she realised what Alex had told her about the entrance to the library. She knew Alex would have to come here and once she'd been how could she not write about it.

Mary felt crushed, she thought she had it all worked out but was fast realising how naïve she was being. "You're going to have to meet her sometime, let's talk to her and see where it goes, when all's said and done she won't print anything that's going to hurt her family, I'm sure we can find a way around this."

"Okay Mary if you think so but remember I feel responsible for the people that live here if they get hurt I don't know what'll happen. For you I'll give it a try. Maybe you should talk to her first but don't tell her too much, see how she reacts before you give too much away. Please be careful, the community needs to be kept safe."

"Ok Jack, then you can meet her and tell her whatever you want. It's up to you. I won't give any secrets away but we need to do something otherwise we can only see each other in secret and I don't want that."

Neither of them knew what else to say, they both appreciated that the other was right but they gradually relaxed into a companionable silence and enjoyed the sunshine, leaning against the wall where it had all begun.

Chapter Sixty Eight

Alex was getting the feeling that there was something going on that she knew nothing about. She'd seen her Nan and even after asking about the man she had seen her with she didn't get an answer and she seemed distracted, Alex felt like she was imposing on something. She couldn't understand why her Nan would be like this, she must know that Alex would have been happy for her if she had found herself a man who she could be happy with. She had felt like she had been almost pushed out of the door and to add insult to injury her Nan hadn't done any baking so there was no cake to eat with their tea.

Alex knew she had to get into work today and get something written up or Charlie would be on the warpath again. She felt like she was getting nowhere with the body in the park story it was just getting more confusing with everything she discovered and still no-one had claimed to know who the victim was. She would have to ring the police station and see if they had had anyone come forward with any ideas. That wasn't such a daunting idea now that she'd received the flowers from Matt and spoken to him. He had rung her last night and apologised and explained that he had just been getting frustrated with yet another body that no one seemed to know anything about. She apologised for her behaviour too. They talked for nearly two hours on the phone and decided to share everything they knew and not let their ego's get in the way. They also made a date.

Alex's personal life was looking up again. She arrived at work and got straight into writing a story that Charlie had left for her to do. She had decided she was going to toe the line from now on and the stories would sort themselves out, she wasn't going to lose her job or her relationship over this story, life was beginning to come good for her. All she wanted to know now was what her Nan was up to. The phone was ringing in her bag, ah speak of the devil she thought.

"Hi Nan."

"Hi Alex, You sound happy."

"I am, Matt and I talked, it's back on and I'm letting the body in the park story go it's been taking over my life too much."

"Well, are you sure about that?"

"Yes it's getting too destructive Nan, it was taking over my life, I couldn't see beyond it and I want Matt in my life, I'll return the books to Tony in the next day or two and it'll be over."

"Ok if that's what you want. Fancy coming over for dinner tomorrow night?"

"I'd love to Nan, will you be baking?"

"Of course!"

Chapter Sixty Nine

Peter was in his shed sorting through all of the rubbish he had collected over the years, it was time to get rid of his old tools and gardening paraphernalia he'd never been much of a gardener, his wife had been the one that loved to grow things, the garden used to be an explosion of colour and smells and a little haven to retreat into when he was overworked or feeling stressed. Now the garden looked terrible since it had been left to him to take care of, he didn't know the difference between a flower and a weed. He would have to get someone in to tidy it up so he could put the house up for sale, the inside could do with some attention too. He picked up an old pair of shears that had rusted on the hook and walked out to throw them in the bin. He could hear the phone ringing as he passed the back door; he ditched his gloves and went inside to answer it.

"Oh there you are, at last. Are you okay?"

"Hello Jack, got anything to tell me?" He grinned as he said it.

"I've been worried about you, where have you been?"

"I just took in some sea air and I feel much better for it, so how did it go?"

"Thank you Peter, I did what you asked and now I can honestly say I've never been happier, she's still amazing and even after I've told her everything about my life she still wants me around. How can I ever thank you?"

"Don't, just be happy. I'll be down to see you in a while just as long as the doctors still allow me to drive, I've got to see them in a couple of days but to be honest I feel okay at the moment."

"Just look after yourself Peter and if you want to come to us we'll look after you, you know that don't you. Don't leave it too long to get here and if it's a problem I'll come to you." Jack could hear himself almost pleading with Peter.

They chatted for a few more minutes and Jack gave Peter his phone number, Peter was stunned that Jack was embracing the twenty first century and overjoyed that things were going well with Mary. It was good for them both to be able to talk.

Peter went back to clearing the shed feeling like he'd done something really good.

Chapter Seventy

The night had come, Jack was happy and relieved that he'd finally got to speak to Peter but was dreading this evening even though he had got Mary on his side, she had organized everything, she was cooking a meal and he would meet Alex and this could be a disaster, what would happen if she decided she just wanted to print everything he told her, he thought he knew the answer to that, he'd be going to prison. This was the biggest thing he'd ever had to do and he was terrified. He just hoped she would be kind because of the others, they hadn't done anything wrong but by association they would be the ones to suffer.

He pulled on his best clothes yet again, he had to smile these clothes hadn't seen the light of day until Mary came back into his life, she was having a hell of an effect on him and he couldn't be happier about it. Mary had asked him to turn up late, she wanted time to get Alex used to the idea of a man in her life. It was already beginning to get dull, the sun was losing its potency and the sky was dimming over the town when he left to make his way to Mary's and he felt himself dragging his feet, his steps slowed the nearer he got to the house, when he got close he could see the house was already lit up, looking warm and welcoming from the outside, he just hoped he wouldn't get a frosty reception.

He tapped nervously on the door; this was a very new experience for him, meeting the family. He forced himself to take a deep breath and calm himself. The door opened and Mary stood there smiling and looking beautiful, he loved how just seeing her made his heart skip a beat. She ushered him in and gave him a slow kiss and told him it would all be alright. He went into the lounge and was introduced to what up until today had been his nemesis; she was a beautiful young woman with blonde hair, petite and dressed in black and looked like butter wouldn't melt in her mouth. She stood up when he entered the room and looked inquiringly at her Nan.

"Alex I'd like you to meet Jack..... Jack Adams" Mary smiled as she watched Alex's face, she looked thoughtful and then the sudden change when the recognition of the name hit her.

"Jack, oh sorry... hello. I don't know what to say, I thought you were lost in the realms of time." She sat down looking confused.

"It's a pleasure to meet you Alex; I hear you've been looking for me?" He sounded a lot braver than he felt.

After the initial awkwardness that can only be associated with strangers, silences followed by shy glances and polite conversation they had a pre-dinner drink and slowly started getting to know each other. Once she got started Alex had a million questions and Mary had to step in more than once to slow things down. They had an understanding that Jack would tell her anything (within reason) that she wanted to know but at the moment it was not for the papers or the police's ears. Alex agreed readily she just wanted to hear the story and find out how on earth her Nan knew him and why she hadn't told her. As soon as she saw him she knew it was the man she'd seen walking with her Nan at the nature reserve.

They stopped talking for a short while to acknowledge the feast that had been laid out in front of them, roast beef with all the trimmings all set out beautifully on the dining table complete with flowers and candles. They hadn't got far into the story and now it was time to stop and appreciate all the trouble that Mary had put in to make this a proper family meal, Jack was touched by the trouble she had gone to. So far everything was very relaxed and Alex hadn't asked any awkward questions. She seemed enthralled by the fact that Jack and Mary had been teenage sweethearts and due to his family they had been kept apart and that was why he disappeared, he had confirmed all the things she had discovered when she had read the notebooks. He knew the evening would get more difficult but right now he was having a very cheerful evening and Mary was glowing with pleasure now they had met and seemed to be getting on well.

After the meal they sat down to talk more, Jack was surprised at how much she knew about his life even down to the design he had left for Mrs Sharp as a thank you for a warm coat, he was touched that Mrs Sharp (Even now he knew her name he couldn't bring himself to call her Eva) treasured that drawing and even wrote a journal. He didn't give her much more of the story but he did confirm the things she already knew, he knew this would get tougher but for now this was okay.

"So what's the connection with the bodies and the baby" She looked him in the eye, the true journalist coming out in her.

He'd just got comfortable with her and then she blindsided him with a question that rocked him to his core. To answer that he would have to tell her everything, he took a deep breath.

"The lady in the park was called Ruby and she was a good friend who hit on bad times and I tried to look out for her, can we leave it at that for tonight Alex, I've had a wonderful evening and I'm not ready to get into this tonight, I promise I will tell you everything you want to know in the fullness of time, just not tonight, this is a story of a life not a two column piece for a newspaper." He hoped she would understand his reluctance.

Mary nodded to Alex who seemed to be thinking his statement over. "Yes of course I can wait, you make my Nan happier than I've seen her for a long time, I won't do anything with this information yet but I would like to hear more when you're ready to tell it." She looked thoughtful and added "Have you really been in love with my Nan for over 50 years?"

"Really Alex, I'm just blessed that we've found each other again."

That seemed to satisfy Alex and she went home happily believing that there was such a thing as true love.

Chapter Seventy One

She felt so happy for her Nan and Jack, it turned out that her Nan hadn't wanted to tell her anything about the relationship because she thought she'd be upset with the idea of her being with anyone other than her Granddad but in truth Alex couldn't have been happier. She did miss her Granddad but her Nan seemed twenty years younger with Jack around and truly happy. She'd liked Jack after the initial shock of who he was had dissipated, that certainly had been a shock but they looked so right together it was hard not to like him, he was kind and incredibly thoughtful. What an amazing life he appeared to have lived too, Alex was looking forward to getting more information on that, he had also confirmed that the notebooks were an accurate account what small part they told and had agreed to meet with her to tell her more of the story. Alex couldn't wait to find out where and how he had lived so secretly for all of these years. She would meet up with him tomorrow and find out more.

Now she also had a name for the body 'Ruby' she was torn about whether to tell Matt or not, maybe she should wait until she had spoken to Jack again at least he might give her a surname and if she was lucky more information about Ruby too.

Chapter Seventy Two

They had barely left each other's side since the meal with Alex and they were blissfully happy, Mary had accepted everything that Jack had told her and decided that looking forward rather than looking back was the best thing to do, after Jack had spoken with Alex they could start making plans for their life together. Their only reservation was to how Alex would report the story as they knew she wouldn't be able to resist the pull of the newspaper, after all it was what she did for a living. Jack had an idea and wanted to put it to Alex when he met her again. He thought he could stop the story coming out for a while at least to give the others a chance to move on if they wanted to. He talked it over with Mary and the decision was made, he just hoped Alex would agree to it.

They spent their time just enjoying each other's company, he had stayed with Mary after the meal the previous evening and this morning they had eaten breakfast together and sat in the garden drinking coffee, he felt so relaxed he couldn't believe all of this was happening to him. They decided to walk over to the tunnel that afternoon and let the others know that he may not be around as much as he used to be but he would be turning up regularly to check that everything was going well with everyone there.

Last night they had been lying in the big soft bed with the softest pillows he had ever laid his head on, Jack had never experienced this before, neither the bedding nor the sensation of another human being offering love and warmth so unselfishly. That was when she had turned her head up towards his and had asked him to stay not just for the night but to stay with her for the rest of their lives and he was only too happy to say yes, from now on they would spend as much of their time together as they could and they wouldn't waste a minute of it. He had to pinch himself, after fifty long years he was moving in with Mary.

He rang Peter and told him the news, Peter was overjoyed and promised to come and visit as soon as his hospital appointments were over. Jack offered to go with him but he said he preferred to do it alone, there were no shocks to be had anymore, he knew what was going to happen to him and all the doctors could do now was to prepare him for it as best they could. Jack was shocked by Peter's acceptance of what was happening to his body. Now for Peter's sake he would try and make as long as he had left memorable.

Chapter Seventy Three

She drove to her Nan's house with her windscreen wipers swinging in a hypnotic rhythm; finally the weather had broken, it was cooler and the rain had come with it, it was not a day to walk anywhere. When she got there Jack was waiting for her at the front door with an umbrella so she wouldn't get wet getting out of her car. So her Nan had found a gentleman in this man, Alex was impressed. They were sitting opposite each other and as she watched him he seemed nervous, her Nan was baking so in Alex's mind everything was returning to normal, Jack kept glancing towards the kitchen as if he wanted to escape the scrutiny and help with the baking. She set her notebook on the table and looked directly at him.

"You don't want to do this do you?"

"No but you deserve the truth, not because you're a journalist but because you're Mary's family, the thought of my life being recorded in a notebook makes me wonder what you will do with the information." He looked at her quizzically.

"I'll write a story about you for the paper and try and find Ruby's family. Where did she come from?"

"I don't really know, we never discussed much about our pasts. Why would we?"

"Where did you both live?"

"Hang on a minute Alex, I have a proposition for you before we go any further." He got up and went to help Mary bring the drinks through to the lounge. "Your Nan and I have discussed this already and think it's the only way we can all get what we want out of this situation."

Alex just sat silently whilst tea was poured and biscuits offered, wondering what Jack was about to spring on her.

"My decision now will affect more than just us in this room. I would like you to consider not writing my story up as a newspaper article." He watched Alex's reactions carefully and at that moment she didn't look happy. "How would you feel about writing it up as a book? There's plenty of tales to fill a book that I will share with you and I would expect you to keep it all secret until the book was published. I have my reasons and if you agree you will see why I'm doing this and that there's a solid, valid reason but if you just want a quick newspaper article I'm afraid I can't tell you anymore than you already know." He felt much better now he had offered her the ultimatum although he was aware she may not be happy about it.

Alex was sitting thinking about what he had just so eloquently said "So it's a book or nothing then? How do I know it'd be worthwhile, it would be a lot of time and effort?"

"It's a story that's never been told, I've been missing for over fifty years Alex, people will be interested and it'd be yours to tell as you wish."

"Alex just think about it, it's a good offer." Mary added.

"Oh, why do I feel like I'm being railroaded here?" She smiled as she said it. "What if there's not enough for a book, could I take it to the paper if I thought that would be the best thing to do?"

"Book or nothing I'm afraid, it's the only deal I'm prepared to do, Sorry Alex but unless it's done properly there could be too much damage."

Alex drank tea and ate biscuits as she thought it over, she didn't as yet understand what damage could be done but what she already had wasn't enough for a good story there were too many holes and a lack of proof, she just needed to work out if it would be worth trying, she didn't even know if she could write a book but she trusted her instincts and she thought it might be worth a try. She looked up at the two expectant faces and smiled.

"Okay, let's write a book."

They all looked at each other and smiled, maybe everything would work out okay after all.

The whole afternoon was taken up with Jack telling Alex all about his childhood, his family and his teenage years, how he met Mary at the amusement arcade and his friend Peter who was the most incredible friend anyone could want. Mary kept providing freshly baked cakes and drinks and chipped in with her own memories of meeting Jack.

Alex was enthralled with the story so far and didn't want the afternoon to end, they agreed to meet up in a few days to really get down to work, Alex couldn't wait but she had a date with Matt this evening and memories of her own to make.

Chapter Seventy Four

Over the following couple of days Jack and Mary started to get into a routine and enjoyed spending their time together. They visited the tunnel and got everyone together and explained why Jack wasn't going to be around very much anymore. All of the community were happy for them and wanted them to visit as often as they could. Jack found Jerry and Mark and went for a walk with them whilst Mary helped the women prepare a meal for that evening. They made her feel completely at home and wanted to share all of her memories about Jack as a young man, they had an enjoyable afternoon together.

Once they were outside Jack explained to his friends what had been happening since Ruby's death and how close they had come to being discovered. They walked to the well and leant against the wall whilst they talked. He also told them about Alex and the book she was preparing to write, they didn't like the idea but Jack explained that it would take some time to get the book organized and would give everyone a chance to leave if they wanted to or to be a part of a new type of life maybe one where they wouldn't have to hide anymore. They understood that there didn't seem to be any other way to deal with the way things had turned out at least this way it bought them more time. Mark looked a little guilty but Jack ignored it and made no reference to his confession. With Jerry and Mark left in charge of taking care of the community Jack felt more relaxed and able to get on with his life. They returned to where the food was being prepared and talked with Mary for a while, they all seemed to like her which was just what Jack had hoped for. Jack and Mary walked home hand in hand, relieved that things were being dealt with to the best of their abilities.

During these couple of days Alex had been seeing more of Matt and they were starting to sort things out and not allowing their jobs to come between them although Alex had not mentioned that she would be writing a book about the body in the park, she wanted to know more about it herself before she could tell Matt anything about what she had found out but she knew she would tell him everything soon. He hadn't put any pressure on her to tell him anything even when they were sitting talking about work over breakfast. They seemed to be getting into their own routine and Alex couldn't remember being so happy in a long time.

Chapter Seventy Five

It was 10am and Alex was on her way to see Jack for more of his life story, she had wanted him to meet her in town but old habits die hard and he still got nervous about going into Charmsbury still aware that someone may recognise him even after all of the time that had passed, so they agreed to meet at Mary's again, Jack was comfortable there, he felt safer talking to her knowing that Mary was just in the next room, after all he had been through he was enjoying feeling relaxed.

She arrived to find a late breakfast laid out for her and lots of questions about her date and how things were going with Matt although the look on her face told them everything they needed to know, she barely stopped grinning. After they had eaten she got her notebook out and started asking questions, Jack hadn't expected her to be so business like, and the last time they had spoken it was much gentler questioning with no added pressure. She recapped some of the things they had spoken about previously and started asking her questions.

"Before we go on Jack where did the baby come into all of this?"

"Ahh yes little Chloe, she was beautiful but quite the screamer. We all tried to help Summer with her but just having the baby had taken its toll on her and she couldn't cope. We had a few women who tried everything to help out but Summer decided she couldn't do it and her pride wouldn't let the other women bring up her baby, we didn't know what she had planned just that one day little Chloe wasn't there, Summer explained what she had done and we had no way of getting the little one back."

"So Summer didn't want her baby?"

"No, she really wanted the baby but the way she was living and being in the community there were no facilities in place for a new born and it was difficult for her, we would have stopped her if any of us had known what she was planning. She was very young, too young to understand what she had given up. She suffered terribly with her decision, I don't think she ever got over it."

"Was she underage or raped?"

"Nothing like that Alex, that baby had been born out of a relationship full of love, Summer was just young and frightened. Do you know where the baby is? What happened to her?"

"Not exactly but I think I could find out if Summer still wants to know. I can tell you the babies name is Lily now and she's in a happy, loving family." She paused for effect. "So Summer was the girl with the tattoo on her hand?" This had not been a question she thought she would get a reaction from.

"Yes the daft girl had seen that design in my room and taken a liking to it, thought it represented our way of life and went and had it tattooed on her. Some of the others wore jewellery with the design on it, it just became our logo of sorts." Jack looked a little sad at this memory "How did you know about it?" He just answered her question but didn't give her the answer she was hoping for.

"It just kept cropping up, when I looked into things there would be your triquetra, I just couldn't find the link." She watched his face and asked him "So where did you all live?"

His face didn't show any emotion "I'll show you when we have the story together, we can save that for a while." They chatted about how he had managed to stay undetected for all of those years and how he met some of the other people he lived with.

"So what about Ruby?"

"She's dead Alex that's why we're here, what else is there to tell." Jack was getting a little tired of the questioning already, he'd told her almost everything he could without revealing where they lived and the bodies and he knew he couldn't skirt around it for much longer. "Sorry Alex, it's difficult with Ruby she was a very dear friend." He explained why and how he had put her in the park.

Alex could see Jack had had enough and it was time she was getting to work, she didn't want Charlie on her back again. They chatted about nothing in particular for a while and she made her excuses to leave she didn't want him to stop talking but the longer it went on the more wary of her he was getting and she needed him relaxed and chatty and most of all she needed him to trust her.

Chapter Seventy Six

It was two days later that Alex returned for more information, Jack was well rested and very much getting used to a more comfortable way of life and being with someone who meant so much to him. Alex could see his contentment as soon as she walked through the door. Jack smiled at her and welcomed her in, he went off to make the drinks whilst Alex and Mary caught up on some town gossip, it made him smile to hear them both laughing about something someone had said to someone else, he thought gossip must be a magical thing for women. The truth was that hearing Mary's laughter made him feel whole. On the spur of the moment he decided to take Alex to the tunnel; she wanted to know where he had lived so it was time he showed her. He took the drinks to them and told them to be ready for a walk when they'd finished their drinks.

The three of them walked over the fields, Alex still not having a clue where they were going. She even mentioned they shouldn't go that way or this way, Jack just smiled and she continued to follow them. They got to the well; Jack was pleased to see there was no recognition in her eyes, so she'd never even begun to work out where he had lived. He stopped and watched Alex as she looked round.

She looked around taking in her surroundings.

"This is where it all started Alex right here at this well."

"Is this where you ran away to? There's a cabin over there, I can just see the roof through the trees."

Jack had to smile. "No, I promise I didn't live in there, that's an outhouse."

"Ewww"

"Why don't you go over to that bush and pick us some fruit, there's loads if you push through to the inside." Jack and Mary stood together smiling as she walked towards the brambles.

The brambles rustled "Wow, what's down there" She asked as she turned back towards them.

Jack explained about the well and the family bible and how he had discovered the entrance. Then they took her inside to show her around, her face showed amazement all the way through the tunnel, the pictures, the wall hangings and the people. She met people that smiled and said hello to her but she was having trouble taking it all in. They went to Jacks room and sat down to relax as he explained how he ended up making his home here for so many years. Every so often someone would tap at the door and pop in just to say hello, Alex was rarely lost for words but she couldn't believe what Jack was telling her.

"So how is it you were never discovered? You're not too far from town."

"No one ever bothered looking I guess."

"How do you get to the library?"

"Come and stay here one night and I'll show you around and take you to the library, I just wanted you to get a taste of the place today." He went on to explain how they lived and about the others that lived there too.

Jack left Mary and Alex to talk and take a look around if they wanted to, he wanted to try and find Summer she would normally be in the garden at this time of day. He walked through some trees which opened out on the other side onto a patch of ground that they had cultivated to grow some of their own food, it had turned out to be a success and Summer was there on her knees collecting the ripened marrows. She turned around sensing Jack behind her and smiled at him. "Hello stranger, nice to see you here." She got up and wiped her hands on her jeans before throwing her arms around him.

"Summer, still getting your hands dirty, I always know where to find you." He wasn't sure whether he should tell her his news or not but it was her business and not his to hide. "I've come to tell you something, it's not much but I've discovered that Chloe is well and happy and I thought you should know." He watched her face as he mentioned the child's name, it was as if she had been slapped. She regained her composure.

"Have you seen her?"

"No, I heard that she has a good family and is loved very much, they called her Lily." He held her whilst she cried against his chest.

Eventually she pulled away from him and looked up at Jack through tear swollen eyes and smiled "Thank you, really, thank you, I think of her all the time; I'm glad she's happy."

Jack made his way back to his room, Mary and Alex had gone to the main room to meet some of the others and were busy chatting about life in the community when he found them. After an hour or so of chatting they left everyone in peace and returned to the house. Alex started to believe there could be a book in this after all.

Chapter Seventy Seven

They settled down for the evening and felt like they'd achieved something today, Alex had gone home early to write up her impressions and the shock of seeing the community, she couldn't believe that they lived under the nose of the town and no one knew they were there. He hoped now that she had seen the tunnel she may start to believe there was enough material for her to forget about writing a story for the paper and he hoped she may do him a favour in return. Jack and Mary had decided to settle down and have a glass of wine in the quiet of the garden whilst the sun went down. Mary went into the house to get some snacks to go with the wine and returned ten minutes later with a visitor. Jack jumped up at the sight of Peter following Mary into the garden. He looked bright and was smiling, Jack was relieved he looked well.

"You're a sight for sore eyes, how are you feeling?"

"I'm fine now, tired but okay."

"So why did you run off, we were all worried about you Peter."

"You're a stubborn old sod and you'd have made excuses forever if I hadn't made it sound like it was my dying wish for you to see Mary. I know I laid it on a bit thick but it got you here didn't it and I got an unexpected holiday on the coast. So it looks like everything's going well here." He smiled knowingly at Mary who was happy to return the smile.

"I'm going to make up the spare room, will you be staying with us for a few days Peter?" She said.

"I'd love to Mary if it's not a problem."

"You'll always be welcome here Peter especially after sending Jack back to me." She went off to sort his room out.

"I'm so tired Jack, I saw the docs and they said I can still drive but I need monthly check ups now and they will soon turn into weekly ones, they want to keep their eye on me, I needed to get away from all of that."

They sat and chatted for a while and Jack updated Peter on the new book that Alex was going to write about the tunnel and the community that grew into it. Mary joined them and they discussed all the things that had gone on through the years with family and friends, there was lots of gossip to catch up on. Mary couldn't believe she hadn't remembered Peter when she had seen him in the café, looking at him now he hadn't changed very much at all, now he was thinner and bald but he still looked just the same to her, his face seemed to belie his age.

After sitting outside for well over an hour Peter started to feel cold and Jack was beginning to notice the constant low coughs that punctuated Peter's speech. They moved into the warmth of the kitchen it was obvious he was getting tired now and they could see it etched on his face, Mary showed him to his room and left him to get some rest, there was plenty of time tomorrow to continue the talking.

They moved into the lounge and settled themselves down on the settee holding hands like teenagers, comfortably sitting snuggled close together they finished their drinks and talked about the old days and the things the three of them had got up to, the fifty years they had been separated just melted away. Jack was so happy to have the two most important people in his life here with him.

Chapter Seventy Eight

This was the day that Jack had planned to take Alex to stay with the community, Mary wasn't joining them this time because Jack wanted Alex to experience a full twenty four hours in the tunnel and see how it really worked, she would get to meet as many of the community as wanted to get involved with the book, he knew some would shy away from it even though she had offered not to use their real identities, Jack knew she would soon come to realise just how damaged some of the people here really were, when that happened he hoped that she would understand why not everybody was as enthusiastic about the forthcoming book as she was. He was looking forward to showing her around and seeing what she made of it.

They arrived at midday and found her a place to sleep, no favouritism, she was given a space in a dorm where any newcomer would be expected to sleep, they weren't going to go easy on her after all she was a journalist and they didn't know if they could trust her yet. Jack didn't step in, he didn't want to interfere with the order of things, this had worked for them for many years and he wasn't running things anymore. She was expected to help with preparing food, helping in the garden and fetching water from the well. She worked hard with no complaints which made the women warm to her. After they had eaten Jack suggested that she get some sleep, he would wake her later to visit the library. Alex had other ideas as she was getting on very well with a couple of the women and they had got into a huddle and were talking about their lives and giving Alex some background information. Jack left them to it he wanted her to gather all the independent information that she could. He went to lie down for a while.

It felt odd to be in his room it dawned on him how easily he had adapted to life with Mary, his room no longer possessed the warmth or the comfort that it once had and he no longer wanted to be alone, he looked at the perfume bottle on the bookcase and thought he should take it with him tomorrow, he wasn't sure he'd be coming back again, at least not to stay.

He awoke at midnight and went in search of Alex, amazingly she was sitting in the dining area still awake and writing her notes up.

"Are you ready?"

She looked up and smiled at him. "I think I've got enough material to write five books, just from being here today, some of these people have had such horrible and sad lives and this place has done such great things for so many of them."

Jack was pleased she could see the good in the community and hoped she would be careful to protect it when the writing was done. He waited whilst she put her books away and led her down the tunnel showing her first the dead end that they had never managed to clear then some of the other rooms that had been rarely used, this would be the closest she could come to seeing the tunnel as it was when he found it. The tunnel started curving upwards a little then they came to the uneven steps, she carefully picked her way up them. At the top Jack showed Alex how he had discovered how to open the door and even though he hadn't used it in years it opened as he remembered with a satisfying click, he removed the panel and crawled into the library, Alex followed behind mentally taking note of everything that he did.

The streetlights let enough light in that Alex could see everything in the library she stood up and turned to see where they had come from.

"Keep down." Jack whispered to her. "We don't want to be discovered just yet."

She ducked down and went off to explore the library by streetlight, he showed her the places where he had found the coat and used to sit to get warm, where the food had been and how he used to wash his clothes in the bathroom. It was only a story for her to follow but he was reliving his younger days, he realised he would never do this again, those days were gone.

Chapter Seventy Nine

Alex woke up the next morning much later than everyone else; Summer had fixed her a basic breakfast of fruit and tea and sat down to talk to her for a while about her life and what had led her to the community. Alex was looking forward to helping out in the garden again before she had to leave, she enjoyed being around the others. Mark walked into the room and sat down opposite them.

"Hi, I have a confession to make." He looked at her with a frown on his face.

"What is it?" She was curious, she'd seen him about but this is the first time she'd spoken to him.

"It was me… I mean the emails and on twitter."

"Ah so you're my John Smith, why did you contact me?"

"I thought it'd be fun to play around and tease you with some information. I shouldn't have done it but I wanted to have some fun." He looked ashamed.

"It's okay, the way things have turned out there's been no harm done."

"You won't tell the world where we are will you? I didn't mean for it to go this far, I've let down the people who trusted me, please don't let anything happen to the community….. It's a good place." He looked like he was going to cry.

"It's fine I'm just doing what Jack wants me to do now, I'm not writing for the paper, its ok."

With that he got up and walked away, Alex felt bad for him but he was right, without him she would never have had a story, she would have given up before she really got started. At least that was one mystery solved.

She went out to the garden and helped Summer with the vegetables, she was beginning to admire these people they had found a great way to live and they seemed so content with this way of life even without the trappings of modernism. She watched Summer picking out the last of the marrows, with her chestnut hair tied back in a loose ponytail and her tanned skin, she obviously loved being outdoors, she thought she would know her anywhere with that tattoo. By mid-afternoon Jack had come to find her and they got ready to leave, a small group had gathered to see them off.

"Can I come back to visit sometimes?" She asked Summer

"I'd love it if you did."

With that they left and went back to her Nan's, she was predictably waiting for them with freshly baked cakes and hugs. Alex was distracted with all of the things she had experienced in the last twenty four hours but managed to get through three helpings of brownies. She had rarely felt so excited about a project.

Chapter Eighty

Jack had a few lazy days, he chatted with Peter, laughed with Mary and kept her close he could no longer bear to be parted from her, she had seemed happy when he bought home the perfume bottle and placed it on her bedside table, it seemed it meant as much to her now as it had to him for the past fifty years. He couldn't meet up with Alex because she had to concentrate on work it appeared that Charlie was loading her up with articles to keep her out of trouble and she was spending all of her evenings with Matt.

He was enjoying his life; he was comfortable, happy and had the people he cared about around him. Peter had decided to stay on for a while, he hadn't returned to the tunnel yet on this visit, Jack offered to take him but he didn't seem too interested he kept saying he couldn't walk that far, Jack thought that was an excuse but let it go.

He decided to take Mary out for a walk and some lunch, as they left the house a young couple from the next house at the bottom of the road smiled and waved at them, Jack smiled to himself, how easy it had become to integrate into normal life. They walked down the road hand in hand, Mary didn't seem to worry about who saw them so he felt relaxed too, he had never realised life could be this easy. He pulled his mobile phone out and dialled Alex.

"Could you meet us for coffee in the Red Bean in your lunch hour?"

"Yes, I can be there in half an hour but I won't have long."

"That's fine I want you to see something."

"Ooh I'm intrigued, see you soon."

He put the phone away and Mary looked at him quizzically. "What's that about?"

"I've just remembered something she should know."

With that they turned the corner and headed to the Red Bean. As they finished their coffee, Alex turned up and Mary went to order another round of their favourite drinks. Jack went up to the counter to get some cakes and stood talking with the head barista for a couple of minutes.

"He'll bring them over." He said to Alex.

"So what was the rush Jack?"

The cakes were put on the table; Alex spotted it straight away and smiled. Mary went to pick up her chocolate cake just before she bit into it she looked at the chocolate curl on the top of the cake that was holding a small diamond ring. She looked stunned. She looked up at where Jack had been sitting a second ago but now he was down on one knee.

"So my Mary I've waited too long, I love you, will you marry me." Jack was astonished at how nervous he felt; it felt like an age that he had been down on one knee.

Mary looked at him with a tear in her eye. "Yes Jack, of course I will, I couldn't stand another day without you."

He reached up and took the ring off the cake and placed it on her finger, he didn't think he had ever been happier or more proud.

Alex was watching all of this with a big smile on her face and in the background the staff started applauding the couple.

Chapter Eighty One

She headed back to work after they had celebrated with coffee and cakes and thought she would look into doing something for Jack and Summer. They had been so kind to her and given her so much information for the book, she was still having trouble taking in all of the things that she had encountered and couldn't believe that the community were so close to town and had never been discovered but there were many more questions she had for Jack. With every revelation that was offered up many more questions arose. She had to write up a copy of the local council's accounts but then she would have a little time to try and sort something out. She sat in front of the computer screen for an hour formatting the tables of the mind numbingly boring figures that the council put out, she tried really hard to make them look more interesting but to no avail, her mind was churning over a way to do something nice for Jack. She sent her print copy to Charlie and decided to go and return the notebooks to Tony.

Tony was pleased to see her and the kettle was on before she could make an excuse to leave.

"Did you find anything interesting in those books?"

"Yes they were really helpful, it should all make a great story when I can write it all up." She paused "Tony, I've decided to write it up as a book now I have so much information, do you think Eva would approve?"

"I think she'd have loved it, the idea that her notes were of any interest to anyone else, she'd have been over the moon just as long as she got a mention." He grinned at her. He had such a genuine smile, Alex really liked Tony it was hard not to and now she had his blessing she could get on with the writing part of this whole project. They chatted for a while and Alex went home to wait for a call from her Mum, by now she would have heard about Nan and Jack and Alex knew she would get the backlash for not telling her about them before now.

She got home and started looking online into more of the history of the building that Edward Heatheridge had built for the love of Charlotte, there wasn't much more to be gleaned just the things she already knew and then it hit her, she reached for her notes taken from Eva's notebooks. He had been catholic with his own Jesuit priest in 1597, she looked online for the information but there wasn't anything to confirm her thoughts, if this was true Jack's community were living in an elaborate priest hole, more of a priest's escape tunnel. It felt right she could feel adrenaline in her system yes it felt very right, that explained why the tunnel was there in the first place and why it had been such a secret place, hard to believe no one else had ever found it but not impossible, that was why the door in the library was so small so it wouldn't arouse suspicion and could be easily hidden, there must have once been a way of opening it from inside the library too. Alex was feeling very pleased with herself when the phone rang, she decided to ignore it she was feeling too pleased with herself to be brought down with family bickering. Then the doorbell rang and she opened the door to Matt who was looking very relaxed and incredibly handsome.

Chapter Eighty Two

He called Peter on his mobile whilst he waited for Mary to finish on the home phone, he needed to check that Peter had got home safely. He could hear Mary's side of the conversation and from what he could hear it didn't sound like it was going well. Mary had phoned her son first which seemed to go well enough and now her daughter to give her the news and he could hear the raised voice through the closed door. Jack was having trouble concentrating on what Peter was saying.

"Jack I'm staying at home for a while I need to speak to the kids and maybe get them to come and stay for a holiday whilst I'm well enough to still do some things with them and explain to them what they should expect, Jack are you listening?"

"Sorry Peter, sounds like our news isn't going down too well this end."

"The family eh, they'll come round don't worry, you're both adults, they'll just have to accept it." He started coughing then managed to get his breath back "Jack it'll be fine, don't worry."

"Thanks, you take it easy Pete that cough is sounding nasty, relax a little, please."

"Relax…. That's all I ever seem to do now!"

"Peter come back here if you're not happy at home."

Mary came through the door with a face like thunder.

"Peter I've got to go I'll ring you back later, Take care Mate." He pressed the off button and turned to look at Mary "That didn't sound like it went well."

"Oh don't worry they'll get over it…. Or they won't it's up to them." She sat down and turned on the television, apparently the conversation was over and Jack knew better than to push her on it. She reached over to find his hand and gave it a little squeeze. Everything would be okay he thought.

Chapter Eighty Three

He had thought about it for days now and decided that he should tell Alex about the bodies and his brother, he knew that was the part she was waiting patiently for and he couldn't put it off any longer it would be the final part of his story and the part that would hurt him most to tell, he hoped she would not go to her boyfriend with the information but knew at some stage she might have to, after all murder was murder and he shouldn't escape punishment however cruel Jonathon had been.

He phoned Alex and asked her to meet him at the only place he could finish telling his story, the community.

He walked out to the tunnel and sat down with his back to the well wall waiting for her, he was nervous this was the only part that could put his future with Mary in jeopardy.

He watched as she came into view across the scrubland and walked behind a hedge so no-one would watch her approaching the tunnel from the nature reserve, she had a confident stride and as she got closer she looked happy, it looked like she was singing to herself, he smiled it was lovely to see her looking like she didn't have a care in the world. She got close to the well, saw him and smiled, he got up to meet her and they went down to his room where it would be private and quiet.

"What's wrong Jack?" She could sense his apprehension.

"Please sit down Alex I have some things to tell you." Jack was touched that she looked so concerned, "Please just listen

Alex, this will be difficult enough and I only want to go through it once."

Alex settled herself into the chair whilst Jack sat perched on the edge of the bed. "You know about when I first came here but when people started joining me here lovely as that turned out to be there were difficult times too, the first time we had a death in the community we didn't know what to do. It didn't seem right to just bury them here there would be people out there in the real world who would be missing them worrying where they were, never knowing." He took a breath. "We... No, I decided that the right thing to do was to put the bodies somewhere where they would be found by the authorities and then they would at least get a proper burial and a chance that their families would get closure if they could be found. The first person in 1979 was Steve, which was his real name, he just didn't wake up one morning it caused a lot of upset but we took him into town and he was found, we never knew if his family were traced or not, I hope they were."

Jack went on to detail the deaths for Alex and told her what he knew about each of the people who had died, where they had come from and if he knew what they were hiding from and finally where he had taken the bodies.

"Those were the natural deaths and believe me I thought it was the right thing to do, I could imagine the worst thing for the families that had been left was that they would never know what had happened to their lost family members. There was one that wasn't natural but wasn't caused here either, a bloke who called himself Will turned up, Peter brought him here as was usual but Will was a drinker and would go out get drunk then he couldn't stop himself from getting into fights, we would patch him up every time it happened and he would swear it would never happen again but sadly it always did, one day he went out and didn't make it back, I believe he was found on the beach having passed out and he never regained consciousness, that would have been back in 1987. He got labelled as a beach bum and I'm not sure the story made much of an impact with the media. In all these years he was the only person we really had any problems with; sure there were spats between people but nothing serious and a couple of times people left us after arguments with others here, we were lucky here it was always the good ones that stayed."

Alex was watching him carefully, noting his reactions he could see the journalist in her now. He made his excuses and went and got a drink, a bottle of water it would have to do, what he really wanted was a beer and to not have to do this at all.

He went back to his room, Alex was still sitting where he had left her and as yet she had not uttered a word. He offered her a bottle of water which she gratefully took. "Alex could we leave this now until another day?"

"Of course, you will tell me about Ruby won't you? She started this for me."

"I will tell you everything I know Alex but some stories are harder than others. Maybe in a day or two I'll feel ready to carry on."

Alex could see he looked exhausted and left any questions that she had for another day. They left together and walked back towards town.

Chapter Eighty Four

Matt was enjoying being around Alex, she was good for him even his workmates at the station had noticed he was happier and more relaxed, finally he felt like he'd found someone special and could see a future with her. He still worried about the work aspect but she seemed to have dropped the body in the park case so there was no conflict anymore the only thing he couldn't work out was why she hadn't taken him to see Mary, they were close in fact Alex was always talking about her, he already knew Mary and he knew that Mary had on more than one occasion pushed Alex in his direction. He thought he might be being a little over sensitive about it but it was playing on his mind.

He drove out to Alex's after work. He wanted to surprise her and take her out for a meal but when he got there she looked tired, she said she had had a long day so he went out to pick up a take away for them, they sat in front of the TV eating curry from the cartons, which he had to agree tasted better than from a plate, she was acting a bit distracted but she insisted there was nothing wrong.

"Why don't we go round and see Mary?"

She glanced over at him "Why?"

"Well, she can always cheer you up and we haven't been to see her together yet."

"Oh some other time, I'm sure she wouldn't be interested in seeing us." Alex said flippantly.

"I'd like to go and see her Alex, I haven't seen her in a long time and I'd like to know she's happy with us." He heard himself almost begging.

"You really want my Nan's blessing? You are strange. I'm not sure she'd want us turning up out of the blue Matt." She was on alert now; the truth was the more she knew about Jack the more worried she was about Matt meeting him. She could see that it must seem odd to Matt that they hadn't been to see her Nan.

"Ok, we'll go, when do you fancy going over?"

"How about now?"

She took a deep breath and mentally crossed her fingers "Ok."

Matt insisted on driving and Alex phoned her Nan to warn her that they were coming.

"You know she's got a man in her life now?" Alex was already trying to make things easy on Jack.

"No I didn't, what's he like?"

"He's a real gent, you'll see for yourself in a minute."

Matt was sensing that she didn't want to go but pushed her into it anyway, if there was something wrong between them maybe he could help. When they got there everything seemed relaxed and normal he didn't understand Alex's reluctance to visit. He had liked Jack and they were pleased to meet him and made him very welcome, Alex had been right about her Nan's cakes too, he would definitely be back. He was shocked when they told him their news.

"So how long have you known each other?" As he asked he cringed knowing it sounded like he was playing the father figure.

"Oh only just over 50 years" Mary said and winked at him.

Well however long they had known each other they were a good fit, it felt like they were made for each other. He was happy for Mary she had been alone for too long she deserved some happiness and Jack certainly appeared to make her happy.

After a couple of hours he took Alex back to his house and made her a cocktail or two before they settled down for what was left of the evening.

Chapter Eighty Five

They woke up late and there was a rush to get Alex home and for Matt to get to work she shouldn't have been drinking cocktails on a weekday and she had the headache to prove it, she was certainly paying for it this morning. She got changed, downed a couple of headache tablets with a glass of orange juice and rushed off to work, after not being in yesterday Charlie would be on the warpath if she didn't come up with a good excuse for being late today, she didn't think drinking too many cocktails the night before would be the right excuse. It turned out okay, Charlie was out when she got in, she settled herself behind her desk and went through the notes he had left for her.

She had been relieved that the previous evening had gone well and the more time she spent with Jack the more she liked him, he certainly didn't act like an average seventy year old, the life he had led had kept him young, they had laughed and joked and Matt seemed to like him and suspected nothing.

She made a couple of phone calls to try to arrange the surprise she had in mind and returned to her work, the least she could do was be up to date with her work for when Charlie got in and her head was finally feeling better.

The new story she was working on was about the decline of the nature reserve, she had to smile to herself, if only they knew what was hiding out there they would get thousands of visitors but her lips were sealed. She enjoyed writing this article up and decided to go and have a look around the reserve for herself just in case there were any plans to do it up, after all the town had been spending money hand over fist on updating the High Street and the park and cleaning up the beach, they may be moving onto the reserve in an attempt to attract more visitors that could potentially be disastrous for the community. On the up side she could flag any work up a little earlier than most and let them know what the plans were. She phoned the local council to see if she could get any information before trekking out there. There was no-one available for comment so all she got was could you please call back tomorrow.

The day had flown by for her and it was nearly time to get out of the office, Charlie walked past her and smiled at her, said hello and kept moving, she was relieved that he hadn't felt the need to check up on her today, she hoped he noticed that she was settling in she had even started putting colourful things on her desk to try and brighten it up a bit although maybe the blue smurf perched precariously on top of her computer monitor may have been a step too far. She had to admit she was starting to like it here.

Her phone rang and she looked at the screen smiling as she took the call, "Yes, ok…. That's no problem, we can do it when? Next Wednesday. Wow that's quick. No, No, it's not going to be a problem. Can't wait, Thanks for setting this up, yes, just text it to me, thanks again." She clicked the phone off and smiled. She went to see Charlie and asked for Wednesday off; he seemed honestly surprised she had asked he was getting used to her just disappearing. Yes he had said Wednesday was a quiet day anyway. She was pleased, everything was coming together better than she could have hoped.

Chapter Eighty Six

He thought it was time to get it over with, he could keep putting it off but that wouldn't do any good he wanted to finish the story for Alex and then it would be up to her to decide what she wanted to do with the information. He had talked it through with Mary but she couldn't help him, she could only support whatever he thought it was right to do, so he decided he should tell Alex and do it now before he bottled out again. He phoned Alex and asked her if she could come over that evening, Mary would cook for them and he would tell her everything and complete the story.

By seven o'clock they were sitting around the table but Jack couldn't find his appetite and his nervousness was putting Alex and Mary off their food too, he helped Mary clear away the dishes and asked her to sit with him whilst he told Alex everything, he wanted it to be the last time it was told.

Alex was sitting down waiting for them to join her. The atmosphere was charged with nervousness, it seemed to take an age for them all to settle down. Jack looked at her with complete openness and started to talk about Ruby, she's been a rebel when she first got to the tunnel but soon became an indispensable member of the community. Jack looked sad as he told his story and with every revelation he looked older, Alex saw how difficult this was for him, then the real story unfolded before her.

Jack took a deep breath and continued "She was lovely Alex, a real live wire you'd have liked her and you would have Mary. There was never anything between us except for friendship; if anyone ever tells you that men and women can't be friends without sleeping together they're lying, I'm living proof. Ruby was like the sister I never had, we were always messing around and playing jokes on people, just normal stuff that friends do. She'd had a tough upbringing most people never talked about where they'd come from and why they hadn't stayed where they were and sorted things out but for Ruby she needed to talk it out and I was her sounding board. You may have heard the stories of the children's homes where the kids were mistreated but her parents had split up and her Mum couldn't control her so the council had sent her to a home in the south of England where the abuse had been mental and physical, I guess that was the cause of her wild streak. The longer she was in the tunnel the happier and more confident she got and she managed to put most of the past exactly where it should be. When the first baby was born to the community she immediately stepped up and helped and became... I suppose you'd call it a nanny, she was brilliant with any kids we had with us." He took a quick break and reached for his cup. "She was happy with us and she felt safe." He stopped again if he had been a smoker that would have been the time he would have had a break but he needed to get this told. "Then we had a visitor in the tunnel one night, it was my brother, Jonathon, he had seen Peter in town and just followed him all day until finally he followed him to the tunnel. I saw that Peter had stood watching everything carefully from the corner of the room. Jonathon had been drinking and was carrying a bottle of whisky in his pocket when he turned up which he regularly swigged from, he started shouting about telling the family where I was and he pushed a few people around and his language was foul, no one retaliated because they had heard that he was my brother and out of respect for me they didn't throw him out. I wish they had... how I wish they had." He looked at his hands, they had started to shake he could feel the old anger or was it terror returning. He noticed Alex was watching his hands too with concern written all over her face. He looked up at her and silently mouthed that he was okay. "Mary darling, could I have a glass of wine?" They stayed silent until Mary came back with the wine and as he took a drink she held his free hand. "Jonathon got louder and more violent and threatened me with the police for hiding out there, I tried to calm him down but when that didn't work one of the younger guys threatened to sort him out outside but Jonathon was too much of a coward for that, he just wanted to humiliate me. We had never got on but some of the things he was saying were really horrible, not that that matters now, he got up and started to make his way out and I thought he was leaving, he was pushing people and even hit one of the women, she was really shaken up, I looked for Peter but he'd gone, I ran in the opposite direction and tried to find him. I needed him to help me get Jonathon out without any more trouble but that was my first mistake as it turns out, I couldn't find Peter, turned out he'd left to try and stop Jonathon before he started shouting his mouth off in public. Whilst I was looking for Peter I heard a scream and turned around, I ran back down the tunnel the way I had come, towards the sound, as I got closer I could hear the scuffle of feet and a muffled voice, I kept moving along the tunnel and there he was.... Jonathon with one hand around Ruby's neck and the other tearing at her clothes, he had her pinned against the wall and as he reached down to undo the zip on his trousers I saw red but was still too far away to stop him. I started running towards him as I watched him rape my friend whilst he laughed manically, I threw a stone at him but it just bounced off him he didn't even appear to flinch from it. I saw a rock on the floor grabbed it and launched myself at him beating him with the rock until he let go of Ruby. He let go of her neck and she slid down the wall into a crumpled heap on the floor, Lizzy ran to her and tried to pull her out of our way and still I kept hitting him with the rock in my hand, he turned on me and I saw the flash of metal in his hand, I jumped backwards and threw the rock at his head as hard as I could, it worked because he didn't come back at me. I turned to Ruby to check that she was okay, she was crying and swallowing air trying to get her breath and she had a huge red handprint around her neck, Lizzy had pulled her clothes back into place and has holding her like a mother cradling a baby, it was a terrible sight. I looked back to register the body of my brother lying on the ground and didn't once feel sorry about what I had done." He reached for his glass and downed what was left of the wine. "I killed my own brother and I'd do it again." Mary filled his glass he smiled at her and took her hand. "After I had checked on Ruby and made sure she was okay and had plenty of people around her to soothe her I went to see if I could move Jonathon's body but it had gone, there was some blood on the floor where he had been, I guess someone had taken him out of the tunnel beyond that I didn't care I was more concerned about my friends and particularly Ruby. She was being well looked after by the other women, I carried her to her room and held her all night hoping that she would be okay, she just lay in my arms like a ragdoll, he had broken her spirit, it was as if it had been the final straw and she had no fight left in her. I cried all night whilst I watched over her. Peter appeared sometime through the night and said he had dealt with Jonathon's body, by that time I didn't really care anymore. The next morning she had seemed brighter and she promised me she was okay and refused to let me take her to hospital, she had a huge bruise welling up on her neck, hip and arms, I knew all of that would heal it was her spirit I was worried about but after a few days she started facing people again, allowing them to fuss over her. I saw the sparks of the old Ruby returning only to be crushed a few weeks later when she discovered she was pregnant from the rape, in the most awful way she was carrying my niece or nephew, she was devastated and confused, eventually she chose to keep the baby after a lot of thought, which I thought was a brave choice. She would have a constant reminder of that awful evening but she thought it didn't matter because the child inside her was innocent. We all settled down to the idea of a new born in the community. Sadly three months later she lost the baby and that was the end of it. She never spoke of the rape or the pregnancy again, it was as if she had wiped it from her mind although she never stopped dealing with the fallout there were many times I would see her sitting somewhere alone quietly crying. I'm still not sorry for what I did to my brother he was a despicable man." He looked up at Alex, she was crying. He leant over and touched her hand. "So you see why Ruby was so special to me, I had to take care of her and make sure no one ever harmed her again and no one ever did."

Chapter Eighty Seven

Alex didn't want to be alone that evening she felt emotionally drained, so she stayed with her Nan and Jack and spoke to Matt on the phone before she turned in for the night, it felt good to hear his voice and at that moment she knew she needed him in her life. She slept in the same room she had slept in as a child when she had stayed with her Nan and Granddad. It had been redecorated but she still thought of it as her room, safe and cosy and filled with love. Still she couldn't sleep, the events in the tunnel in 1981 were playing over and over in her mind, she would never have believed that Jack was capable of murder but the circumstances had been awful, who knew what any human being was capable of when certain conditions presented themselves, the thing that worried her the most was that she would have to tell Matt, this was an open case even if it was 34 years old and she had the information to close the case. She didn't want to give Jack over to the police but how could she write the book that Jack had asked her to write without giving him up. She tossed and turned all night and eventually got up at 5 o'clock because sleep wasn't going to happen for her that night. She went downstairs to make herself a coffee and found Jack sitting at the kitchen table staring into his own cup of coffee.

"You couldn't sleep either" He said as he looked up at her. "Sit down and I'll make you a drink."

"What am I supposed to do with this information Jack? I've been trying to work it out all night."

"You do whatever you need to with it, I did what I did and I always knew that eventually I would have to pay for it."

"If I write the book I'm going to have to tell Matt, I don't want to but he'll find out when the story gets published."

"Alex just do your best to protect the others in the community, they've done nothing wrong. I'll pay for what I did and your Nan understands that too."

"Oh no Nan, how am I going to tell her that I've got you arrested?" Alex put her head in her hands.

"Don't worry she knows, we've discussed it and she'll understand." They sat in silence for a while just drinking coffee and watching the sun come up.

Mary joined them two hours later and sensing the mood of despair in the kitchen she hugged Alex, kissed the top of her head and set about making some breakfast. She didn't need to discuss anything with them she knew the decisions that needed to be made next.

Chapter Eighty Eight

Jack had understood what had to happen and wasn't surprised when Alex rang him later in the day to arrange a meeting for them all. She had decided it would be easier on him if they met at her Nan's, going to the police station was just more than she herself could cope with, this was going to be difficult enough for everyone involved and she hated doing it, this could tear everyone's lives apart but there didn't seem to be another way. She had decided to leave it until the end of the week, which would give Matt a chance to read all of the notes before they all met up. It was going to be a rollercoaster of a week but she wanted to give Jack the chance to see everyone he needed to before she involved the police.

She spent the day writing up her notes so they were clear and explained it as well as they could and she wanted to show Jack in the best possible light, she was beginning to see him as a permanent fixture in her family. She was sitting in her lounge with her feet up on the coffee table. Under normal circumstances she loved the weekends, little to no work and plenty of time to relax but today she felt restless and worried, how could she do this to her Nan, the only alternative was to not write the book but this had haunted Jack for decades but could she let it haunt her in the same way? What an awful decision to make, tell the world or tell no one. Maybe now Jack was almost a septuagenarian they would go easy on him, no, she knew that couldn't happen either, a crime had been committed and someone had to pay. She was beginning to wish that she had never taken on this book idea.

She phoned Matt and asked him to come round that evening and to bring a take away and wine; it was going to be a long night.

She went back to her notes and scribbled away with only one break when her phone beeped with a location for Wednesdays meeting the next thing she knew there was a knock on the door.

"Matt, you're early."

"No you told me to come round after work."

She looked up at the clock, the whole afternoon had passed her by and she hadn't even realised it she had been so engrossed in her work. She poured a glass of wine for each of them and took the food through to the lounge and set it down on the coffee table, sweeping her notes to one side.

"What are you working on?"

"Just some notes that I want you to read, let's eat first I don't want to think about it for a while."

They sat down and enjoyed their meal and wine, for the first time in twenty four hours Alex started to relax and almost managed to push her distress out of her mind, the wine was definitely helping with that.

"You've been a bit distant tonight, are you okay?" Matt asked.

"Yes I'm fine."

"Is this about whatever you're working on?"

"Yes but can we leave it for now? You'll get to read it soon enough." She smiled at him but mentally kicked herself, she had bottled out when she had the perfect opportunity to open up to him and she couldn't bring herself to do it.

Chapter Eighty Nine

Jack had spent the day milling around the house but was getting very bored, he was restless and he needed to do something. He rang Peter and told him what had been happening, Peter was totally against the idea of the book and the police being involved, he wanted to know why Jack felt the need to sabotage his new life just as he'd found real happiness. Jack couldn't come up with an answer that would have kept Peter happy all he could say was that it was what he felt he had to do; after all it wasn't Peter who had to carry the guilt. Peter mentioned that he would be visiting in the week, so at least Jack would be able to talk to him face to face and try to make him understand.

He was still feeling restless so they decided to go for a walk over to the tunnel, Mary had thought it may calm him down and she was sure that she could keep herself amused for an hour or two with the children. They ambled over towards the tunnel and Jack had to admit Mary had been right it felt good to be out here again even if it was only for a visit, he went to find Mark and Jerry and chat about his decision with them, he thought he should keep them updated on what may happen when the police knew of the existence of the tunnel. He was amazed at how understanding they were he had expected them to be trying to talk him out of his confession but they seemed to understand and said they would speak to the others and explain so if anyone wanted to leave they had the chance to get out before the police arrived. Jack could have hugged them for being so understanding.

When they left the community to walk home Jack had felt much more relaxed and more certain that he was doing the right thing. They even decided to go out for dinner at a local pub and vowed to make the most of the time they had together. He was touched that Mary had understood why he had to do this; he knew it was harder on her than it was on him. They sat in a cosy corner in the pub and held hands like teenage sweethearts.

Chapter Ninety

It was Monday evening before Alex handed her notes reluctantly over to Matt, they had been at his house for a change and he had cooked her a lovely meal, she thought herself lucky to have found a man who could cook as she herself was no great shakes in the kitchen, the cooking gene in the family had skipped her generation. They sat talking over the dining room table and she handed him a notebook with all of the information in it.

"Please read this Matt, it will answer a few things you wanted to know but for me please do not share it with anyone else for a few days, if you read it you will understand why." She looked away unable to meet his eyes.

"What's this about? Whatever it is it's been on your mind for over a week."

"It's what you wanted to know about the body in the park case and much more. Please just read it and we can all meet up at the end of the week and talk it through." She looked up at him. "Promise me just one thing."

"I don't know what this is about but you're worrying me Alex, are you in trouble."

"No, I just need you to promise me that you won't do anything with this information until the end of the week, it's important, Please Matt."

"Okay, Okay I'll read it and we can talk about it on Friday." He was starting to get worried about what was in the deep red covered notebook that Alex was so eager he do nothing about. Her face told him it was serious.

Alex felt like she shouldn't stop the night with Matt, it didn't feel right and he would want to start reading her notes. She called a taxi and could see from Matt's face that he was worried about her. "Don't worry, I'm fine it just feels like I've ruined the mood of the evening now. I'll see you when you've read that." She nodded in the direction of the book. "Call me when you're ready." She gave him a kiss and swallowed back the lump in her throat; that was it she'd done it, she'd ruined everyone's lives and now they were all going to have to wait and see what Matt would do next. He looked confused as she left, all she could hope was that he would tread carefully with the information.

She got home and curled up in her own bed alone and cried until she finally fell asleep, emotionally exhausted.

Chapter Ninety One

Matt was sitting at his desk, it was only Tuesday and already the week was turning into a nightmare, he had sat up all night reading the notebook that Alex had given him and he couldn't believe what he had read, he came into work early to start going through the unsolved cases she had outlined and putting names to the victims and casualties.

He had read and reread the notes, it was hard to take it all in and he understood why she had asked him to not tell anyone else, this involved Alex's new family member, who had been the perfect gentleman and funny and kind and Mary loved him and now Alex had given him the ammunition to blow all of that happiness out of the water. All the facts in the notes checked out against his unsolved cases, he thought he may be able to get around having to charge Jack for the death by natural causes cases although that could be difficult as he had admitted to moving the bodies but he couldn't ignore the case of Jonathon Adams. Alex had asked him to hold off from doing anything until Friday and for her he would do that. He thought he should ring her and see how she was feeling. He got hold of her on the first ring "Oh Alex." was all he could say.

"I had to tell you Matt, please be as kind as you can to everyone, this is so horrible." That was when her voice broke and she openly wept down the phone, he felt so helpless.

"I will, try not to worry, I'll come over tonight and we can talk, okay."

Alex agreed and that took a weight off his mind at least he may be able to hold onto her, he was worried this would drive them apart but her still wanting to see him was a relief. He was worried about Mary and Jack too and he really hoped that they were holding themselves together, this was going to be a rough ride and he wasn't sure that he could keep Jack out of prison. He was also struggling to believe anything about a tunnel outside town, Alex hadn't given a location just mentioned that that was where the crime happened, he would have to ask her later about that. He was also hoping that after he could speak to Jack he may be able to put this together as a self-defence case.

He leant back in his comfortable chair and decided the next step was to go back to the earliest case and see if the names she had given him could help them find any relatives, it wouldn't be easy some of these cases were years old but it would keep him occupied until he could see Alex later and assure her he would do everything he could to make life as easy as possible on all of her family.

Chapter Ninety Two

Alex had seen Matt the previous evening and filled in some of the gaps for him but refused to give the location of the tunnel she had told him that that information he would have to get from Jack. She had woken up this morning next to Matt and for the first time begun to think that things might just be alright and just maybe they could all get through this.

Today she had a lot to do and first she needed to make a few phone calls and make sure everything was still on track for this afternoon. She was sitting in the kitchen with a steaming mug of coffee in front of her and made her calls, she was relieved to hear that it was all going to plan so she went and had a shower and phoned her Nan and told her that she would pick them up at 2 o'clock.

First she needed to go to the tunnel and pick up Summer, she would bring her back to the flat to get ready before they picked her Nan and Jack up. It all went to plan until they got back to the flat and Alex realised that Summer didn't have anything with her apart from what she stood up in and there was no time to hit the shops. Summer constantly asked what was going on but didn't seem too reluctant to go along with something she knew nothing about which made Alex's life easier. Alex went off to find something for Summer to wear, she was a similar height to Alex but a little thinner, nothing a belt wouldn't put right. Alex found a lovely outfit for her and pushed Summer into the bedroom to get ready, pointing out make up and mirrors and told her to use whatever she wanted.

Half an hour later Summer walked into the kitchen and Alex was stunned, when she had stripped away the jeans, t shirt and the old black boots she looked completely different. Alex had to consciously close her mouth aware she was gawping at Summer. She had put on the black trousers that Alex had sorted for her but obviously gone looking for something more comfortable than the blouse and jacket and had found a light grey cashmere jumper with kittens on the front that had cost Alex a week's wages, she looked stunning in it and Alex could only look on and wish she had looked half as good wearing it. Summer had picked out a pair of flat black pumps to go with it and she looked perfect and she had chosen not to bother with any make up, she had just piled her hair up on the top of her head in a very bohemian up do, a loose piece of hair fell across her face and made her look simply elegant.

They went off to pick up her Nan and Jack who were ready and waiting when they arrived, they piled into her little car and drove through town and out the other side, it wasn't far away but Alex was feeling nervous she really hoped they would all be happy with her surprise. She pulled up outside a café overlooking the coast and they went inside and ordered drinks, Alex was bombarded with questions which she still refused to answer, the bravado in her voice wasn't matching up to the butterflies in her stomach, she just prayed that she had done the right thing.

Thirty minutes later she saw them arrive Patty leading the way towards the café, Alex smiled as they came through the door, Jack and Summer couldn't see them as they were sitting with their backs to the entrance but the look on Alex's face told them that their surprise was here. Four adults and a child walked slowly towards the table, Summer turned to see what

Alex was smiling at and she was dumbstruck, walking towards her was a smaller, younger version of herself, she was looking at her daughter with the couple who had adopted her and two other people, at that moment she didn't care who the adults were she just gazed at the girl who was only a little shorter than she was herself. Everyone seemed to be waiting with baited breath to see what would happen. Summer stood up and smiled at the adults and held her arms open to the child. Lily moved towards her, glanced at the tattoo on her hand and walked straight into her embrace. All Summer could manage was "Hello Lily" by the time the hug was over there wasn't a dry eye around the table. Everyone was introduced and Alex was surprised how kind and easy going Steve and Angie were considering their daughters real Mother was sitting at the same table. Alex, Mel, Patty and Mary went for a walk to leave the others talking and hopefully arranging something for the future, Jack stayed with Summer to add support for her and he was every bit as emotional as Summer was. Everyone seemed so happy and it all went so well even Lily seemed to just accept what was going on and take it all in her stride, these people were meant to be together and Alex was glad she had interfered. There were hundreds of questions asked of everyone and Alex hoped they would have a lifetime to answer them for each other.

Alex had had a good afternoon too. Patty and her ever smiling face and contagious laugh had been just what she needed to get her through the rest of the week; the four of them had walked along the beach and caught up with the town gossip. Laughing and joking like old friends and promised to do it again very soon.

They had returned home and chattered about how everyone was and Summer was so happy she couldn't thank Alex enough, Lily's family had welcomed her with open arms and wanted to make regular dates to meet up and Lily had been a chatterbox who made everyone laugh. It had all worked out perfectly, now the day was over Summer said she would walk back alone, she needed time to take in everything that had happened today and before she left she gave Alex a hug that almost squeezed all of the air out of her. Alex added that she should keep the jumper, it looked so much better on her. Alex went into the house with her Nan and Jack and for a short while they forgot about everything in the future and talked about the day they had just had and enjoyed the moment.

Chapter Ninety Three

The days this week had flown by and so much had happened but now the day he was dreading was here, in a few hours Alex and Matt would be here and his story would reach its inevitable conclusion. He had spoken to Alex a few times but she hadn't mentioned anything about what Matt had thought of it all. Peter should have arrived yesterday but he had phoned to say one of his kids was staying over longer than expected and Jack couldn't blame him for wanting to spend every available moment with his family, Peter had his own problems to worry about but Jack knew he would miss Peter's support today.

For now Jack just wanted to sit in the garden with Mary, who he could see was trying very hard to keep her emotions hidden, she didn't want him to see how much she was hurting but Jack understood because he was feeling all the same emotions. They sat in the morning sun holding hands, much of the time they sat in silence as all of the talking had already been done and there was nothing left to say, they each understood what was about to happen perfectly.

At eleven o'clock there was a sharp knock at the door and when Jack opened it Matt was stood in front of him dressed in his police officers uniform, this was no social call; his face was sombre and just behind him stood Alex. They settled themselves into the lounge and everyone sat there looking at each other.

"Jack you know why I'm here?" Matt started the conversation very formally.

"Yes Matt, let's get on with it." He replied both Alex and Mary sat back quietly watching the proceedings looking from one to the other like an incredibly enthralling tennis match.

"Alex handed me a notebook at the beginning of the week we need to go through it and confirm or deny its contents."

They got down to work immediately going through the story a passage at a time, it seemed to take an age to sort it all out but eventually Jack confirmed that all of the notes were correct and added a few more details for Matt to check out.

"Now I need to know precisely where this tunnel is Jack."

"I'll take you there. I don't want police turning up there mob handed, there are good people living there who have had a bad deal in life. If I take you they'll be more likely to talk to you and see there's nothing to be worried about, they tend to have an understandable fear of authority."

"Anyone still there that would have been around that night?"

"Yes a few but they'll tell you the same as you already know, it's the truth."

All of them went walking across to the nature reserve, Matt looking on like this was some kind of joke "Where are we going? There's nothing out here."

"Matt I wish I had a tenner from all the people who had said that to me." He managed a smile.

Mary and Alex trailed behind a little just watching what was unfolding in front of them until they got to the well and Jack and Matt stopped.

"Okay where now?"

Jack motioned for Alex and Mary to go on ahead and when they disappeared into a bramble bush Matt thought they were playing with him.

"Come on Jack I don't have time for this."

"Just follow where you saw the ladies go either it'll be very crowded behind that bush or there's something there." A little backchat helped Jack feel better.

Matt walked into the brambles and couldn't believe his eyes, he looked to the entrance and slowly, unbelievingly went inside. The people he encountered moved away from him until they saw that Jack was just behind him then they slowly returned to what they were doing.

"Please ask anybody you see about that night, they will tell you what they know, I'd rather you did it on your own so I can't be accused of trying to influence anybody." With that Jack turned around and went outside and sat by the well. He would go and see Summer later he knew Alex would be with her now discussing everything that had happened on Wednesday. Whilst he sat and thought he was aware of Mary settling herself down next to him, he put his arm around her and they sat and waited for Matt to finish his investigation.

An hour later Matt appeared and nodded that he was done Mary went and found Alex and they walked back to the house. Matt was constantly saying how amazed he was that he had never known that the tunnel existed and curious about how they lived. Jack was tired and had had enough he just wanted to go home.

They sat down again in the lounge and Matt explained that he would take all the information back to the station and piece it all together and he would do the best he could for Jack. Then he left.

Chapter Ninety Four

The following morning two police officers turned up at the door and asked Jack to accompany then to the station, which he did with no argument. At the station he was formally charged with the murder of Jonathon Adams, the police wrote out a form and told him to empty his pockets, take his belt off and any jewellery he had and leave it at the desk. What little he had on him was sealed in a bag, the paperwork signed and taken away. He was led down a brightly lit corridor and put in a cell, they asked him if he had a solicitor if not they would appoint one for him. They shut the door of the cell and left him alone.

He had a bed, a sink and a toilet he sat and looked at the plain grey walls and silently prayed to a god he had never believed in that this would work out okay in the end.

Later in the day an officer came to get him, informing him that Inspector Jones would be interviewing him and his appointed solicitor Mr Black was waiting to speak to him before the interview. He told the solicitor everything he had told Matt or maybe he should be calling him Inspector Jones under these conditions, his solicitor seemed confident that he would get bail with it being an old case and Jack had given the police all of the details. Inspector Jones came into the room and asked if they were ready for the formal interview. He made Jack feel as comfortable as he could as all the information was rehashed yet again for the benefit of the recording equipment.

Mr Black asked Matt to allow Jack to be released on bail, Matt thought about it and knowing Jack a little, agreed whilst admitting it was very unusual for a murder case but he knew Jack was no flight risk and no risk to the public, he thought it was the least he could do for Jack although he didn't say that out loud. Conditional bail was agreed on the terms that Jack must live at Mary's house until the court date. Jack gratefully agreed.

Chapter Ninety Five

When he returned to Mary's house she was there with Alex keeping her company, they had been waiting for the phone to ring to find out what was going on and they both ran to him and flung their arms around him when he walked in the door. The relief was palpable. After he had brought them up to date on what had happened at the station he phoned Peter to let him know the outcome and see when he would be visiting next he also wanted Peter to speak to Matt and confirm that he was the one who moved the body. Peter agreed to come down the following week. They all began to relax, Alex rang Matt and thanked him for the bail, and then she announced she was going off to meet him so they could catch up with their lives which had been put on hold, whilst the body in the park case was being taken care of.

Jack and Mary were left alone to enjoy some time together they didn't think they would get. For the first time Mary started to talk about their wedding. That weekend they visited the tunnel once to let the others know what was happening but they didn't stay long, just long enough to learn that Summer was going to meet Lily and the family again the following week. They were truly happy for her.

For the rest of the time they did nothing that didn't include both of them, they were inseparable and making memories with every spare minute.

Alex and Matt managed to work out the awkwardness of what had happened between them and started to move forward with their relationship, they were growing to trust each other more every day regardless of their work circumstances. It seemed for the time being that everyone was more relaxed now the truth was out.

Chapter Ninety Six

His mobile rang.

"Hi Jack, I haven't heard from Peter and he's not answering his phone, is he with you?" It was Matt.

"No Matt he said he was going to visit but he hasn't got here yet." Jack's stomach lurched, immediately he thought the worst, could his friend be dead at home, he berated himself for even thinking that.

"Let me know when you've heard from him will you, we need his statement and I don't want to have to send police officers to his house if it's not necessary."

"No problem."

He hung up immediately and tried Peters number, surprisingly Peter answered on the second ring. "Hi just checking you're okay Pete, Matt said he couldn't get hold of you, what's up?"

"Nothing, I've missed a couple of calls, just haven't got to the phone in time, I'm up to my neck in paperwork trying to sort out the house."

"Can you ring him Pete, he just wants to confirm some aspects of my story, it shouldn't take above a couple of minutes and when are you coming down?"

"I'll be with you as soon as I can Jack, it'll be good to catch up, lots to talk about."

Jack let Peter get back to his paperwork and got on with his day until his phone rang again.

"Jack can you come down to the station please." Matt's voice sounded odd, but Jack didn't ask any questions.

"Sure, 30 minutes okay?"

"Yes, see you soon."

Mary drove Jack to the station and waited in the reception area whilst he was taken to an interview room. Matt came in about ten minutes later.

"Sorry to drag you in but I needed to clarify something you put in your statement."

"Okay, what's the problem?"

"You told me that you beat your brother with a rock and then threw it at his head and that was when he died."

"Yes that's right, I told you that straight away." Jack had no idea what was going on.

"Jack I've been checking the post mortem records and what killed Jonathon wasn't a blow to the head, he was stabbed in the neck with a sharp blade which severed the carotid artery. Jack you didn't murder your brother, someone else did." Matt smiled at Jack.

"What do you mean? All these years I believed it was my fault and someone else did it. No you must be wrong I saw him with my own eyes." Jack was stunned and didn't know what else to say except "Are you sure Matt?"

"Jack we may need you back for a court hearing but I can assure you the worst you did was throw a well-aimed rock that made him black out for a minute or two, the blow to the head was not life threatening. Go home Jack, celebrate and I'll sort everything out this end."

Jack sat there on the uncomfortable chair in the dull sparsely furnished room hearing all the words but unable to take in what Matt was saying, it would slowly sink in he was sure but all he knew was that he had to go and tell Mary to get on with the wedding preparations, he was a free man.

Chapter Ninety Seven

He decided everyone needed to let their hair down after the tension of the last few weeks so Jack and Mary booked a room in the local pub. 'The King's Head' was on the outskirts of town and easy for everyone to get to, they invited everyone, Jack phoned Peter who promised to come down for it, everyone in the community couldn't wait for a party, Tony and Sandra, all of Lily's family, Patty, Mary's Daughter and family were invited and they were pleased to finally be meeting Jack and of course Matt and Alex would be the guests of honour. The food was arranged and they could relax and enjoy themselves, then Jerry asked if they could put the music on for the evening which Jack thought would be a wonderful idea. Everyone was looking forward to it and they all needed some good old fashioned fun.

A couple of days before the party Matt phoned Jack. "I've managed to track down Ruby's Mum, I've just spoken to her and told her where Ruby has been since she ran away from the home."

"Wow she's still alive, I didn't expect that."

"Yes and she wants to talk to you, she's old now and sorry for the way things turned out, will you meet her?"

"Yeah, I will, she should at least know what a wonderful woman Ruby was. Just let's have the party first then I'll meet with her okay?"

So with that organised the only thing Jack had on his mind was what would happen to the community after the news got out. "Matt, what'll happen to the tunnel?"

"I'm keeping it quiet for now, I don't think there's any need to reveal where it is just now, do you? But it'll come out eventually, there's nothing I can do about that."

"Thank you Matt. See you Saturday."

Chapter Ninety Eight

It was the night of the party, Jack was nervous what if nobody turned up, he really hoped Peter could make it he needed some fun at the moment, and he had said he would be there but Jack couldn't reach him by phone today. They got to the Kings Head early to make sure everything was in order the room was full of food and the band were setting up, there were smiling faces everywhere. Both Mary and Jack started to feel a buzz of excitement. By seven o'clock people started turning up and everyone looked pleased to be there, Alex turned up saying that Matt was following on and Summer turned up with Angie and Lily, Jack had never seen her so happy. The evening was fantastic, the band was really stepping up to the mark and everyone seemed to be having a great time, Patty was the life and soul of the party which surprised no one. Jack met Mary's daughter which had been nerve-racking for him but she was a lovely woman and he could see where Alex had got her good looks from, they looked more like sisters than mother and daughter. He was relieved that she seemed to like him despite the amount of time they took to tell her what they were up to. Matt turned up at about nine o'clock apologising and muttering he'd had some work he had to finish but he soon got into the party mood. Everyone had fun, the only down side to the evening was that Peter hadn't turned up and Jack was worried about that, he hadn't spoken to him all day and hoped he was okay, he went outside telling Mary he needed some fresh air and tried to phone Peter again, still no answer. He thought he may need to go and see him in the next few days. He sat down on a bench outside the pub in the cool fresh air and got lost in his thoughts about how quickly his life had changed and how suddenly he had so many people around him that cared about him, he wasn't used to this but it felt good, he was suddenly aware of someone sitting next to him he looked across to see Matt.

"Hi, didn't hear you."

"You were miles away." Matt replied.

"Yes I guess I was, I was thinking about Peter."

"Ah well, I don't want to spoilt your evening but that's the reason I was late tonight Jack."

"Why, what's Peter go to do with….." It suddenly hit Jack and his hands went to his head. "No."

"Yes I'm sorry Jack, it was Peter that murdered your brother, we arrested him as he turned up here tonight, and after he was arrested he told us everything."

"Why would he do that? I don't understand" Jack was close to tears.

"He had hated Jonathon, apparently he thought he would make you go back to your old life and then he wouldn't see you anymore, Jack he was jealous plain and simple and what he saw Jonathon doing that night was enough to make his actions justifiable and he wouldn't get the blame because you threw the rock and he knew you believed you had done it. He liked the power he had over the community, it made him feel important and you all were reliant on him."

"No, but we weren't..." Jack stopped what he was saying and thought about all of the times it had been Peter who decided who came to the community, Peter who drip fed the money. "But he was my friend…"

"Yes he was but he was also jealous of you and your ability to live the life that he wished he had lived, can't you see Jack if you believed you had killed your brother he was your best friend keeping your darkest secret and you would always go to Peter for everything you needed."

"And I did…. he knew me better than I knew myself." The realisation hit Jack hard.

Epilogue

The case against Peter was taken before the court, Jack had to attend to give evidence which he considered the most difficult thing he had ever had to do, whatever Peter had done he had always taken care of Jack and he was having trouble believing the reasons why Peter had done it. He would always find it difficult to replay that experience in his mind, hearing the prosecution team rip his friends' character apart, he still couldn't believe Peter had been trying to control him and everyone else in the community. Peter was found guilty of the murder of Jonathon Adams and sentenced to ten years custodial sentence, which due to his failing health he had to spend in hospital being watched over around the clock. Jack visited him twice after the court case and asked him why but Peter just shrugged his shoulders and said "You had everything, whatever you touched turned to gold, I wanted to be just like you Jack." Jack never really understood that but accepted what he said, after all, this was no time to argue with him. Seven weeks after sentencing Peter died.

Alex spent eight months writing the book exactly as Jack had requested her to, it was an instant success thanks to the media following Peter's case and scrutinising every part of it. But it was her that had the inside scoop. She continued to work at the Daily News; Charlie had been over the moon when she said she wanted to stay, he knew she could have moved on, as she'd had several offers from other papers.

Alex and Matt had been hailed as the golden couple locally and their relationship was going from strength to strength.

Summer left the community and found herself a little flat close to Lily, she was slowly being integrated into the family, Alex and Jack still met up with her quite often.

Some people from the community are still there, many moved on when knowledge of the tunnel became public, those that stayed now spend their time showing groups of tourists around, explaining how they all lived and still live there.

Jack still visits Ruby's Mum when he can, she's in a home now but loves to see Jack and hear about the happy times that Ruby had with the community. It took her a long time to get over how things had turned out between her and her daughter but accepted that she was to blame and was thankful that Ruby had found happiness, surrounded with good people that cared about her.

Jack and Mary are planning to get married in the spring of 2017.

Acknowledgements

I would like to thank everyone who took the time to read 'The Community' I know how precious your time is and I'm grateful that you gave me some of yours.

I would also like to take a moment to thank everyone who told me I could do it and to my husband who gave me as much quiet time as I needed to complete the task. Kath and Mom for the inspiration, Kirsty Prince for her amazing proofreading skills, there are too many people to mention individually but you know who you are, Thank you.

If you would like to contact me or leave a review you can use Facebook page 'SC Richmond'

Or leave a message for me at
scrichmondauthor@yahoo.co.uk